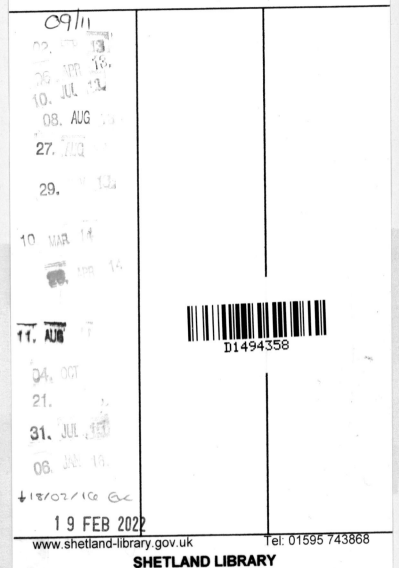

Penelope Bush trained and worked as a tapestry weaver, but always knew that one day she would write. She lives in West Sussex with her husband and son and elderly cat. She hides away in an old caravan to do her writing, where the only distraction is the occasional pheasant wandering past. Now and again, the family reclaim the caravan and it is towed down the coast to Dorset, where many happy hours are spent looking for fossils.

Also available by Penelope Bush:
Alice in Time

'I absolutely loved this book. It's
an exciting page-turner that 99%
of teenage girls will love.'
Chicklish

Penelope Bush

Diary of a Lottery Winner's Daughter

PICCADILLY PRESS · LONDON

For Phil and George

First published in Great Britain in 2011
by Piccadilly Press Ltd,
5 Castle Road, London NW1 8PR
www.piccadillypress.co.uk

A catalogue record for this book is available
from the British Library.

ISBN: 978 1 84812 139 3 (paperback)

1 3 5 7 9 10 8 6 4 2

Printed and bound in Great Britain by
CPI Bookmarque, Croydon CR0 4TD
Cover design by Simon Davis
Cover illustration by Susan Hellard

Mixed Sources
Product group from well-managed
forests and other controlled sources
www.fsc.org Cert no. TT-COC-002227
© 1996 Forest Stewardship Council
FSC

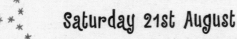
Saturday 21st August

Hooray, we're going on holiday after all! Auntie Sheila has finally decided that we *can* have the caravan. Mum is not best pleased that it's such short notice.

It's not that I'm desperate to go on holiday or anything. I can think of better ways to spend a week than holed up in a tin box with my smelly (sorry, Spencer) brother and my diva (not sorry, Chelsea) of a sister. It's just that Mrs Harper, my English teacher, told us to keep a diary for one week of the summer holiday and so far NOTHING has happened that I could possibly write about.

The reason she wants us to do it is because we've been reading *The Diary of Anne Frank* and when we all groaned and said there was nothing to write about she said, 'Nonsense, Anne Frank was in hiding and stuck in three rooms for two years and she found plenty to write about.'

I cried when I read her diary. It was all that stuff about what she wanted to do in the future; when everyone who reads it knows that she doesn't get to have a future. I felt uncomfortable reading it because I couldn't help thinking that her private diary was no longer private and that it had now been read by literally millions of people. I tried to imagine how I'd feel if this diary was published and read by loads of people. Which of course it won't be, unless I die tragically.

This diary is secret, not even my best friend Lauren knows about it, so I'm definitely not sharing it with Mrs Harper or the whole of the English class. I'll write a separate diary for my homework when we're on holiday in Weston-super-Mare.

As for my own diary, I've filled eleven exercise books so far, which is funny considering nothing exciting ever happens. Anne Frank would be proud of me.

I mean, so far the highlight of my holiday has been the sleepover at Lauren's, which is hardly exciting reading, even if we did make a gory blood pact by pricking our fingers with cocktail sticks and swearing to be 'Best friends, best friends whatever, best friends forever.' My finger still hurts a bit and I can't help thinking that the whole thing was totally pointless because of course we'll be friends forever – we don't need a blood pact to prove it.

Apart from that, the only other thing I've done is help Mum out with one of her cleaning jobs. The Bings live in a really big house and Mum cleans for them. She's not supposed to take me with her but the Bings were on holiday in the south of France.

When we got there, Mum said I could watch television. First I wandered around the house wondering what it would be like to live in a place like that. It isn't far from our own house on the Ratcliffe estate but it might as well be a million miles away.

Mum was in the kitchen doing what she calls a 'deep clean', something she always does when the owners go away on holiday. I couldn't imagine what there was to clean. The whole place looked immaculate, like something out of a magazine. There were two enormous cream leather sofas in the living room hidden under a mass of cushions. The television was more like a cinema than a television. I found the controls on the coffee table but didn't dare switch it on. What if I broke it? Mum and Dad would never be able to afford to get it fixed. I didn't want to sit on the sofa. It didn't look very comfortable and I'd mess up the arrangement of cushions.

I wondered if the Bings would like to adopt me. That way I'd get a bedroom all to myself instead of having to share with Chelsea. Charlotte Bing has quite a nice ring to it.

In the end I said I'd help with the dusting. That was before I realised just how many ornaments the Bings had. The place was stuffed with them; they were on every surface. I'm positive that if Mrs Bing had to do her own dusting she'd have taken the lot down to the charity shop years ago.

3

Upstairs, in the Bings' bedroom, was an enormous wardrobe. It wasn't one of those fitted ones; it was antique-looking, all glossy, dark wood with carving on the doors. One of the doors was slightly open and when I went to shut it I had a peek inside at Mrs Bing's clothes. There were all these fur coats in there.

I'm a bit ashamed of what I did next but I couldn't help myself. I'm twelve, for heaven's sake! I'm going to be in Year 8 when I go back to school next week and I really should be trying to develop a more mature attitude.

Anyhow, I'd never seen a wardrobe like this before and I had to try it, just once. I pushed my way through the fur coats, holding my breath (not because of the overpowering smell of mothballs but because I was really wishing it would work and I'd find myself in Narnia). Then I bumped my nose on the back of the wardrobe.

As I was dusting the shepherdesses on the mantelpiece I gave myself a lecture on how stupid I was to even try such a thing. The truth is though that for a moment I really believed it might work.

I've always believed in magic. When I was little I was convinced that the minute I left the room all my toys came to life. It used to take me ages arranging them so they were all comfortable and not trapped in the toy box. For ages I thought it was true because when I'd go back up to my room they'd have moved.

I'd leave my Barbie sitting on the window sill, looking out of the window so she didn't get bored when I was at school.

But when I got home she'd be sitting in the middle of the room with Spencer's old Action Man. I spent hours creeping up the stairs to the bedroom door and then flinging it open, hoping that I'd catch them moving. Eventually Spencer took pity on me and told me that it was Chelsea who was moving them about. She never let me forget it.

And then I was convinced that there were fairies living at the bottom of the garden and I used to leave bits of food out for them. And then I thought there were Borrowers living behind my dolls' house and I'd leave useful things lying around for them to find, like old matchboxes and paperclips and bits of string.

Obviously, I don't believe in that stuff any more, although I do make sure that Trevor, my bear, is always tucked up in bed before I go to school.

Maybe the Narnia thing didn't work because the fur coats were all fake.

Lauren says I shouldn't let my imagination run away with me but I can't help it. It makes life more interesting so I don't always tell her what I'm thinking any more, because now we're twelve some of it does sound a bit crazy. I think that's why I started writing a diary; because it got too much keeping it all to myself. It doesn't matter if I say what I really think in this diary because I'm the only one who's ever going to read it.

Anyway, I went with Dad to pick up the caravan because Mum said she couldn't trust herself to be nice to Auntie

Sheila after all the hassle she's caused us. And besides, she has to sort out cover for her cleaning jobs next week.

We've borrowed Auntie Sheila's and Uncle Ron's caravan every summer for the past five years. It's the only way we can afford a holiday, only this year Auntie Sheila said we couldn't have the caravan because she was going to sell it. She wants to buy an apartment in Spain instead. And now, just days before the last week of the summer holidays, the caravan hasn't been sold and so we can borrow it after all.

Mum thinks that Auntie Sheila was just being awkward because she's so up herself.

Auntie Sheila brings out the worst in Mum.

It's just as well Mum didn't come, because when Auntie Sheila found out we weren't going away until tomorrow she wouldn't let us take the caravan. She said she wasn't having it sitting outside our house overnight – 'Not on the Ratcliffe estate' – because by the morning it would either be stripped bare or have drug dealers selling out of it.

Dad didn't argue so I guess he was thinking she was probably right.

I was doubly glad Mum wasn't there because I know she would have pointed out to Auntie Sheila that the biggest drugs bust in our neighbourhood was when Mr Lowe was caught selling stuff out of his burger vans and he doesn't even live on our estate. He lives not that far from Auntie Sheila. But then Auntie Sheila would have started on about our neighbours, the Gardners, who are definitely all criminals and proud of it.

Actually they live two doors down and most of them are locked up at the moment. They're rubbish criminals. Barry Gardner, the father, tried to rob the post office. He had a fake gun and wore a crash helmet but he didn't count on Mrs Barnes being in there picking up her pension. She poked him with her umbrella and said, 'Can't you read, young man? It says no helmets to be worn in this shop. Take it off immediately.' So he did! And he'd forgotten to wear gloves, which was unfortunate because he'd got *Barry Rules* tattooed across his knuckles.

Spencer says it's better to live next door to thieves because they're never going to rob their neighbours.

We'll have to go back in the morning to pick up the caravan.

Mum and Chelsea are downstairs having a huge row. Chelsea is refusing to go on holiday with us. Mum says if she thinks we're leaving a sixteen-year-old alone in the house for a week she's got another think coming. Chelsea says she is not missing Sophie Jacobs's party because she's got a hot-tub and everything and Chelsea has just spent all her savings on a brand new bikini (white with gold beading) and a lot of bloody use that's going to be in Weston-super-Mare!

Mum told Chelsea off for swearing and told her it was a family holiday and as she was part of the family she was coming whether she wants to or not. Mum is funny. If she thinks that's swearing she ought to come and stand in our playground for ten minutes. Her ears would curl up and drop off.

Chelsea is now sitting on the top bunk, having stormed up to our room and slammed the door. She is ignoring me and madly texting all her friends. I wish Mum hadn't insisted she comes with us. I would definitely be a lot happier if she stayed behind.

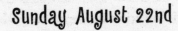

Sunday August 22nd

Just got back from picking up the caravan.

Uncle Ron is really nice. He gave me a big hug and said he thought I'd grown loads since he last saw me. This is a huge lie of course, because I'm still as small as ever. I know because I measured myself yesterday on the bedroom door and I'm the same height that I was last month and the five before that. Sometimes I panic that I'm never going to grow any more and I'll be four foot five forever. But it was nice of Uncle Ron to pretend. He's Dad's brother and I wish he'd never married Auntie Sheila. I wish he'd married someone really kind and happy like my mum.

I stuck by Dad the whole time because I didn't want to be left alone with Auntie Sheila and Pom Pom. Spencer says Pom Pom is the spawn of the devil. She's a sort of poodle but really small. Her fur is white but it's so tightly curled you can see her skin through it so she looks pink. She's the meanest dog on the planet.

Once, when we were there, Auntie Sheila had put on this big tea with cakes and biscuits and stuff. 'Showing off,' Mum called it. I was about to tuck into a lovely piece of cake when Pom Pom lunged at me from beneath the table and grabbed the cake out of my hand. All Auntie Sheila saw was Pom Pom scoffing a whole piece of cake at my feet and getting butter icing all over her stupid white rug. She had a right go at me for feeding unhealthy rubbish to her precious Pom Pom. Never mind that she was happy for us to eat it.

Spencer nearly choked to death trying not to laugh. Auntie Sheila sent us out into the garden and told us we couldn't go on the lawn. When we got outside we laughed until I was nearly sick and Spencer had to take his glasses off to wipe the tears away. We went and sat on a bench at the end of the garden and Spencer said I was lucky the horrid beast hadn't taken my hand off – although if it had, we could have made Auntie Sheila have it destroyed. He said 'Destroyed' in his Darth Vader voice which started me laughing all over again until I realised that I hadn't got to have any cake. It was okay though, because Spencer had stuffed the big pocket on the front of his hoodie with loads of yummy things, so we sat at the end of the garden scoffing them until it was time to go home.

Spencer is definitely the best big brother in the world, even though he smells a bit sometimes and his voice keeps going up and down at the moment. I try not to laugh when it happens, because he never laughs at me for being small. And besides, Chelsea teases him about it enough for two people.

So I had to hang around while Dad and Uncle Ron talked about really boring caravan things and hitched it up to our car.

I was sitting in the caravan, trying to imagine what it would be like if it was ours and I could move into it and not have to put up with sharing a room with Chelsea, when Auntie Sheila and Pom Pom climbed in. She'd brought me a glass of orange juice. Pom Pom started sniffing my feet, which is hardly surprising since my trainers used to belong to Spencer so there was probably a lot there for him to sniff.

Auntie Sheila isn't very good at talking to children. She puts on a funny voice, sort of cheerful sounding but really fake. She'd probably be better at it if she had some kids of her own but she and Uncle Ron never had any. I couldn't stop staring at her lips. She had so much red lipstick on and it had sort of run into the lines around her lips which were probably there because she smokes so much. I was staring so hard, it began to look really funny and I had to pinch the back of my hand to stop myself from giggling.

So after she'd said, 'Charlotte, how lovely to see you,' there wasn't much else to say. She likes to drag out the 'ar' in Charlotte, so it's Chaaaarrrrlotte. Mum says it's because, according to Auntie Sheila, I'm the only one of us kids who has a proper name. Dad insisted his first-born was named after his football team, Chelsea, and Spencer was named

11

after the striker that scored the most goals that year. Mum said when it came to me she put her foot down and said she was going to pick my name. I think Dad had run out of football ideas anyway.

Personally, I think Charlotte Johnson is far too long a name for such a short person. Mum put Amy in the middle to compensate and I'd much rather be called Amy because it's so small and suits me better. But then I'd be called Amy Johnson and she was a very famous aviator who went missing when her plane ended up in the Thames during the War. I know because I looked her up after Grumps kept making flying jokes every time he saw me.

Auntie Sheila was looking me up and down and I could see that she was disappointed with what she saw. Her hopes that I might fit into her idea of what a girl should look like were dashed by my lack of girlie clothes. She probably thinks I have to wear my brother's cast-offs because we're poor or something; but the truth is I choose to wear them. I had on one of his old rugby shirts and some khaki commando-style trousers which I have to roll up at the bottom on account of my size. And his trainers, of course. Auntie Sheila was not impressed. She sniffed a bit and then left.

I opened the window a crack in case it was me she was sniffing, although I'm sure it was just her way of showing her disapproval. That's when I heard Uncle Ron telling Dad that Auntie Sheila wants to get rid of the caravan because he likes to go and watch the football and drink beer in there.

Uncle Ron said there was a couple round yesterday

looking at it, but he managed to put them off by telling them there was a slight problem with death-watch beetle in the roof but nothing that a good fumigation wouldn't sort out, which might get rid of the flea problem at the same time. He said he'd never seen anyone move so fast in such a confined space and they'd gone before Auntie Sheila had even come out from the house.

Uncle Ron told her that the couple had taken one look at the caravan and said it was too small. It's a five-berth so Auntie Sheila was suspicious. He doesn't know how much longer he'll be able to stop her from selling it. That means this could be our last holiday in the caravan. In other words, this could be the last year we get to go on holiday.

It only took forty-five minutes to get to the campsite. Dad gets nervous pulling the caravan so we never go further than Weston-super-Mare.

I think Mum is beginning to wish that she had left Chelsea in Bristol. I know I am. She's making everyone's life hell. She's in a massive sulk and when she does say anything it's in a really grumpy voice. Spencer and I are trying to involve her because we're hoping she'll snap out of it soon, but if it goes on much longer we might have to go off without her.

Not that there's much to do round here.

Last year we stayed on a campsite that had an indoor swimming pool and a bar and a games room and evening entertainment. This year we had to take what we could get at such short notice so this campsite is pretty basic. It's got toilets and shower blocks, a laundry room and a shop. That's it. But you can walk into Weston-super-Mare from here so I suppose that's a plus. At least we're not stuck out in the countryside with nothing to do.

We walked along the sea-front and went down onto the beach for a bit but it was too cold to really enjoy it. I was dead offended when Dad asked me if I wanted a ride on the donkeys. How old does he think I am? I did sort of wish I could go on them, though. It's a family tradition, having a ride on the donkeys. And now we're all too old and it made me kind of sad.

We found an amusement arcade and Dad gave us some money for the machines and he and Mum went to sit out at the café next door. Spencer spent most of his on the big shooting games and the bike racing machines. I like going on the Penny Falls and I could spend hours just slotting my money in. Chelsea stood about looking bored and wouldn't have a go on anything.

When we got back to the caravan Chelsea nabbed the top bunk. There's a curtain that we can pull across. Mum and Dad sleep on the sofa which they make into a bed at night. There's another seat that makes into a bed for Spencer. Dad says he'll put the awning up tomorrow so we'll have more room.

Monday August 23rd

Dad was up really early, wrestling with the awning. It's up now so we had breakfast in there. We decided to go to Wookey Hole today, but when Mum went to get Chelsea out of bed she claimed she was dying from period pains and couldn't go anywhere. In the end, Mum decided she'd be okay on her own for the day and we went without her. I think everyone was a bit relieved really. At least we don't have to put up with her long face all day. So I didn't tell anyone she was lying because I know she had her period two weeks ago. I haven't started mine yet but I do know that no one has one every two weeks.

Spencer and I had a real laugh at Wookey. We all went down into the caves and Spencer and I hung around at the back laughing at the tour guide because he looked like a troll and we thought he'd probably been born and raised in the caves. After that we all played crazy golf and then Mum and Dad settled down in the café and Spencer and I went to the amusements. We were way too old for most of them but we had a laugh at the magic mirrors. I especially liked the one that made me look really tall with legs up to my armpits. Then we looked at all these old penny arcade machines they had in there. Those Victorians had some funny ideas of what's amusing. At least three of them showed executions – hangings, heads being chopped off and even an electric chair. I thought they were creepy and horrid. Spencer couldn't get enough of them though, so I left him to it and told him I'd meet him in the shop. Then, just as I was leaving, I saw a dusty old machine hidden away in the corner of the room. In the glass case was the top half of a gypsy woman behind a crystal ball. It was a really bad, unconvincing model made of papier mâché which had sort of disintegrated because it was so old and it made the gypsy woman look like she had a hideous skin condition, but something about the way the machine was all alone in the dark corner drew me to it.

Let Gypsy Ginny tell your Fortune. She's Never Wrong.

I thought about going to get Spencer so we could have a laugh together, but I was worried that he'd just dismiss it as complete rubbish and I wanted my fortune told. I had my twenty pence piece out and was about to put it in the machine when I noticed that it said, *Please insert One Penny*.

Wow, that's cheap, I was thinking as I scrabbled about for a penny in the bottom of my pocket. I was about to slot the tiny coin into the big slot when I stopped and realised it must mean an old penny. I was about to give up and go away but then I thought that a two pence piece is nearly the same size as an old penny. What was the worst that could happen? I'd put my two pence piece in and it would do nothing? It wasn't exactly going to break the bank. But then, when I'd dropped it in, I panicked that I was going to jam the machine and get into trouble. I looked around and sure enough there was an attendant lurking at the other side of the hall. I slid into a shadow and tried to look invisible until he'd gone.

Just then, the flaky old woman inside the cabinet sprang to life and with one jerky movement, like some sort of zombie, she flung her hands up to the crystal ball. My heart did a double backflip; I hadn't expected the thing to actually move! Then the machine spat out a card from a slot at the bottom. I'd just grabbed it when the attendant came up.

'You can't use that one,' he said, stepping between me and the machine. 'It doesn't work. It's going for restoration.'

I slipped the card with my fortune on it into my pocket and sidled away.

Tuesday 24th August

Today was a bit boring. Dad and Spencer went fishing and Chelsea, now miraculously free of any period pains, went off with a girl called Zoë she met on the site. Zoë is the daughter of the site managers and they live in a bungalow near the entrance. They didn't invite me to join them so Mum and I had a quiet day reading. I tried to text Lauren but when I pressed the send button it said I didn't have enough credit, so I settled down with *The Secret Garden* instead. I skipped the beginning bit where Mary's mum dies because it always makes me cry.

In the afternoon I made a start on my diary homework and because nothing much happened today I wrote a load of facts about Weston-super-Mare that I got off some leaflets Dad had picked up at reception. I'll cut some of the pictures out and stick them in when we get home. It makes me laugh to think I'm writing a fake diary as well as my real one.

Wednesday 25th August

Today seemed like it was going to be even worse because it rained really hard all day and nobody could be bothered to do anything. We were all beginning to get on top of each other and, when Mum got a board game out, Chelsea instantly disappeared to see Zoë.

The rest of us played the board game and then cards until lunchtime. I thought it was great fun and wanted to carry on after lunch, but Dad retreated behind his newspaper and Mum got out her word-search book. Spencer grabbed his Gameboy and flopped down on the bottom bunk because his bed had been made back into a seat. I was about to complain and tell him it was my bed but decided I couldn't be bothered, so I climbed onto the top bunk. It was covered in Chelsea's random junk; magazines, make-up and chewing gum littered the sleeping bag. I started to push everything down the end so I could get comfy with my book. A tube of lip gloss fell off and Spencer caught it.

'No thanks,' he said, passing it back up. 'I'm trying to give it up.'

'How about a copy of *Hello* magazine?' I offered. 'Or a piece of chewing gum, or . . .' I sniggered, 'how about a photo of Josh?'

'Let's see,' Spencer said and I handed him the photo I'd found under Chelsea's pillow.

Spencer and I like to have a laugh at what a typical teenager Chelsea is. I'm not officially a teenager until my next birthday when I'll be thirteen. I'm secretly terrified that I'll wake up one morning and start behaving like Chelsea. This would mean I'd start arguing with everyone, sulking, going off in a huff and texting my friends all day. Not to mention the time I'd spend thinking about my clothes and what all the boys in my year at school think of me. Spencer says that it's a myth that *all* teenagers behave that way and that he doesn't think I'll be like that. God, I hope he's right.

Spencer said I go too far the other way and, whereas Chelsea only ever thinks about herself, I spend way too much time thinking about everyone else and worrying about them and that I really need to lighten up. I'm sure he's right because Grumps said something similar to me a while ago. He said I had an old head on young shoulders.

Spencer handed back the photo and I replaced it under Chelsea's pillow so she wouldn't know we'd seen it.

'What gorgeous specimen of manhood do you keep under your pillow?' said Spencer, groping about under there.

'What's this?' he said, holding up the card from the arcade machine. It must have fallen out of my pocket when I got undressed and ended up under there. I made a swipe for it but I wasn't quick enough so I had to explain about the creepy machine I'd found at Wookey Hole the other day.

Spencer looked at the yellowing card and read, '*Gypsy Ginny says: Your wishes might come true so be careful what you wish for.*'

We were both silent for a minute while we thought about what this meant.

'I wish it had said I grant you three wishes, or something,' I said to Spencer. 'That's just pointless. What does it even mean?'

'I think it's some kind of Chinese proverb,' said Spencer, who always seems to know everything. 'It means you might think you know what you want but what you want isn't necessarily what's good for you. You know, like King Midas who wished that everything he touched would turn to gold. And then he couldn't eat anything because his food turned to gold and when he hugged his wife she turned to gold as well. It was a real bummer.'

I listened to the rain beating down on the caravan roof and said, 'Well, that's just stupid. I know exactly what I want. For starters, I wish we could afford a better holiday, somewhere hot and sunny, and I wish I had a bedroom of my own and I wish you weren't the cleverest boy in school so that you didn't keep getting beaten up.' I added the last bit because I didn't want all my wishes to be for myself.

Spencer looked offended. 'I don't keep getting beaten up,' he said.

'Okay then, picked on,' I amended, to make him feel better.

Thursday 26th August

This morning Chelsea announced that she was going out for the day with Zoë. They were going to the cinema and she'd see us later, she said. I was really put out that she didn't invite me to go along.

I've found out that Zoë is only thirteen so she's nearer to my age than Chelsea's. Chelsea is always going on about how I'm too young to hang out with her. It's really not fair. It's only because Zoë looks sixteen because she's so tall and wears so much make-up. Mind you, even if I wasn't so small and didn't look about ten, Chelsea probably still wouldn't want to hang around with me, just because I'm her sister.

At least it had stopped raining so, after breakfast, the rest of us went into Weston-super-Mare. It was a bit depressing. The pier was closed because it had burnt down and was still being re-built.

After lunch we were mooching around the shops when I spotted Zoë. I followed her into Dorothy Perkins expecting to see Chelsea as well but Chelsea definitely wasn't with her. In the end I went up to Zoë and asked her where Chelsea was.

'How should I know?' she said.

'But I thought you two were going to the cinema together,' I told her. That flummoxed her. I could almost see her brain working. Should she deny all knowledge of knowing where Chelsea was or should she go along with the pretence?

In the end she said, in a bored sort of voice, 'We went to the cinema but we couldn't agree on what to watch so Chelsea went in on her own.'

'Oh yeah,' I said, 'Chelsea loves going to the cinema on her own.'

Zoë looked so relieved, I had real trouble not laughing.

'There you go then,' she said and wandered off. I watched her go, wondering what the hell Chelsea was playing at. She would never go to the cinema on her own. Chelsea never does anything on her own if she can help it. She likes an audience too much. She's always surrounded by friends.

Then it occurred to me that she doesn't seem to have one special friend. Not like I've got Lauren. I think she'd like Sophie to be her special friend but Sophie's got Amber and the truth is Sophie is way out of her league, not that it stops Chelsea trying to get in with that crowd. She only got invited to Sophie's party because Josh asked her . . . then it hit me. Of course! It was today that Sophie was having her hot-tub party. Chelsea must have gone to it. She could easily have caught a train back to Bristol.

Mum and Dad are going to go mental when they find out. But then they'll only find out if I tell them. So I'll just have to keep quiet and hope that Chelsea doesn't get carried away by the party and gets back before they notice.

It was a close one. About six o'clock I could see Mum getting twitchy. She kept looking at the clock. Dad wanted to eat out but Mum said we couldn't go out in case Chelsea came back and couldn't get into the caravan.

'Did she say what time she was going to be back?' asked Dad, looking at everyone. I shrugged.

'I'll find out,' said Mum, picking up her phone and starting to text. Chelsea only communicates by text on her phone; she never talks to anyone on it. I really hoped she had it switched on. Dad gets grumpy when he's hungry and I could see he wasn't about to have his evening ruined by Chelsea. A minute later Mum's phone bleeped.

'It's okay,' she said. 'Chelsea's gone bowling with her friend and she'll see us back here. She says can we leave the key in one of the shoes in the awning.'

Dad wasn't too happy about that, he's very security conscious, but he agreed in the end because he wanted his dinner.

There was a heart-stopping moment when we went past the site managers' bungalow and Zoë came out carrying a bin bag. Luckily she turned her back to put it in the bin and nobody else was taking any notice anyway.

When we got back after eating fish and chips on the sea-front, Chelsea was in bed pretending to be asleep. But there's something wrong because I can hear her snuffling and she doesn't have a cold. I wonder what happened to make her so upset. I'll find out tomorrow.

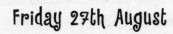

Friday 27th August

Because it was the last day of the holidays, we went out in the car and ended up at Glastonbury. It had me and Spencer in hysterics; it had loads of witchy shops which sold weird things that you'd probably need if you were a witch. There were clothes shops selling velvet lined cloaks and black, floaty dresses. There were shops which sold cauldrons and ceremonial knives and one shop sold dried powders and unspeakable things in jars. It was seriously weird. I was pretending to myself that I was a Hogwarts student wandering round Hogsmead and I got so carried away I almost asked for a butterbeer when we went to a café for lunch.

The weather cleared up a bit so Dad and Spencer decided to climb Glastonbury Tor. I was tempted to go with them but I wanted to find out what had happened to Chelsea yesterday.

Mum said she wanted to look round the abbey and Chelsea groaned and said there was no way she was going to spend time staring at a pile of old stones. I would have liked to have gone with Mum because they say King Arthur is buried there and it's kind of romantic. But I said I'd go with Chelsea who wasn't too pleased but didn't argue. It was like she was too depressed to bother. She walked off as if I wasn't there and I was left to trail behind. Eventually she sat down on a bench and got her phone out. She was checking it for texts but I don't think she had any. After a while I asked her what was up.

'Nothing,' she said, as I knew she would.

'I know where you went yesterday,' I told her, 'and it wasn't to the cinema with Zoë. You sneaked off to Sophie's party.' That gave her a shock.

'Do Mum and Dad know?' she said, all panicked. But it was obvious they didn't or all hell would have broken out.

'Of course not,' I said. 'So what was it like then? Was it really good?'

Chelsea didn't say anything. I was about to tell her that if she didn't tell me all about it, I was going to tell Mum and Dad where she'd gone (not that I would, but Chelsea didn't need to know that), but when I looked at her, I saw that she was trying not to cry. A tear had escaped and was about to fall off the end of her nose. I didn't have the heart to threaten her when she was in that state and I was just resigning myself to the fact that I'd never know what had happened when she said, or rather squeaked, 'I got to the party – I was going to surprise Josh – but when I got there I found him in the hot-tub with Sophie and they were . . . they were . . .' She couldn't carry on and had got all snotty, so I rooted around in my pocket and found an old tissue. Chelsea took it gratefully which just goes to show what a state she was in.

In case I was in any doubt about what exactly Josh and Sophie were up to in the hot-tub she finally managed to blurt out, 'He was snogging her! I'm never talking to him again. Or her.'

I did feel sorry for Chelsea because she's fancied Josh forever and he had invited her to the party after all, so I didn't think it was unreasonable of her to be upset. Well, upset is a bit of an understatement – devastated, more like.

'And then Sophie was really mean to me and was laughing and said what made me think that Josh would be interested in me . . . and she said my bikini was chavvy and cheap-looking . . . it cost me thirty pounds!' This started her off sobbing again and I couldn't blame her. That's a whole month's pocket money for her. And now she'd never be able to wear it again because of the bad memory.

'And then she told me to get back to the council estate where I belonged.' She'd stopped crying now. Her face had set into a furious mask.

'Living on the Ratcliffe estate doesn't make me a bad person,' Chelsea said.

I suspect the real reason Sophie was mean had more to do with Josh than where Chelsea lives. Sophie has been perfectly happy to let her hang out with them – until Chelsea started to show an interest in Josh. That's when Sophie decided Chelsea wasn't good enough. I wondered if I should point this out but decided that Chelsea wouldn't want advice from a twelve-year-old.

'Just forget about it,' I said. 'She's not worth it.'

I've never understood why Chelsea wants to be friends with that crowd in the first place. I mean, they go skiing in the winter and abroad to places like Bermuda in the summer. What did she have in common with them?

Chelsea was back to normal now, apart from a red nose, and we could see Mum coming.

'Don't you dare tell anyone any of this,' Chelsea said quickly. I just hoped that by the time we all got back to school it would have blown over.

The last night of the holiday was much better. We had a barbecue and Dad put some music on and showed us how to dance – which meant that really he was showing us how *not* to dance – but we didn't tell him that. Chelsea was even in a good mood which was a huge relief; only I couldn't help worrying that it was because she was planning her revenge on Sophie.

By bedtime we were all finally in the holiday mood, which was a pity because we had to get up early the next day and pack up to go home.

Saturday 28th August

In the car on the way home, Mum and Dad were talking. I think they thought we were asleep. Spencer was sitting on one side of me with his head back, snorting occasionally and breathing out salt and vinegar crisp smells. Chelsea was on the other side, her head at an uncomfortable angle and dribble coming out the side of her mouth. Not her most attractive look. I had my eyes shut so that I didn't have to see these things. Typical. They had the window seats and I was stuck in the middle with nothing to do and the battery on my MP3 player had run down. Bored, bored, bored.

'I think they're getting too old for these caravan holidays,' said Dad.

'I know what you mean,' said Mum, 'but it's either that or going to stay with my parents.'

There was a silence while they thought about that and

I smiled to myself. Not that there's anything wrong with Grandma and Grandpa exactly. They live in Norfolk, though, which is miles away, so we don't get to see them much. I always get the feeling that they don't approve of Dad. I think it's got something to do with the fact that we live in a council house. Whatever, they don't come and visit us because there's no room. At least, that's their excuse.

'It's not even as though camping is a cheap holiday any more,' Dad complained. 'There's the price of petrol for one, then what they charge to sit in a field is just daylight robbery, if you ask me. Not to mention what we paid out in food and tea trying to keep warm on the sea-front. And the only thing the kids wanted to do was put money in those machines . . .'

Then they were quiet for a bit, and I wondered if I ought to say something so they knew I wasn't asleep because I felt like I was eavesdropping on a private conversation. I didn't bother though, because then they started talking about stopping somewhere on the way home so Mum could buy her weekly lottery ticket. In fact, it nearly turned into an argument, because Dad didn't want to stop with a great big caravan stuck on the back of the car, but Mum insisted and said if he went to the Tesco outside the town he'd be able to park easily and she needed a few things for next week's packed lunches and she didn't want to go out again once she got home. I could practically hear Dad grinding his teeth but he didn't refuse like I know he wanted to. Mum and Dad hardly ever argue. They know when to give and take.

But Dad was obviously annoyed, because he started going on about what a waste of money the lottery was and how people were fools for doing it because they were never going to win and it just raised false hope in people. He said it was always the poorest people who spent the most on it because they were the most desperate. He hated it when he heard people say, 'Oh well, when I win the lottery . . .' because he wanted to shout at them that they were never going to win it and they should be spending the time they were thinking about what they'd do with the money they were never going to have by thinking about how they could improve their lives 'in reality'. He was definitely off on a rant.

Mum said she agreed with him, but the problem was she had these numbers every week and she just knew that if she stopped doing it her numbers would come up. Dad said that's how they got you, and how would she ever know the numbers had come up if she didn't check them.

That's when I did fall asleep.

I woke up in Tesco car park. Mum and Chelsea had gone in because Chelsea never passes up a chance to shop. I wished I'd gone in as well though, because Dad was still going on about the lottery.

When Mum and Chelsea got back in the car, Mum was really quiet and Chelsea looked even more sulky than usual. I was worried that they'd had a row in the shop.

When we got home I helped Dad and Spencer take everything out of the caravan. Chelsea had gone straight inside and put the television on. I thought it was really unfair that she didn't have to help but Mum, who would have made her, had disappeared. By the time we'd finished I was wondering where Mum had got to. Normally she'd be in the empty caravan, giving it a serious clean before it went back to Antie Sheila's.

Spencer was in the kitchen raiding the biscuit tin and Chelsea was slumped on the sofa. It's amazing how everything gets back to normal so quickly after a holiday. I decided to go round to Lauren's and went upstairs to tell Mum. The bedroom door was shut and I was about to go in when I heard Mum give a sort of screech. I hesitated, then the door was flung open by Dad.

'I'm just going round to Lauren's,' I told him. 'See you later.'

'No, wait,' said Dad. 'Mum and I will be down in a moment. Go and put the kettle on; your mum's got something to tell you all.' I looked over his shoulder. Mum was sitting on the bed with the phone pressed to her ear.

I joined Spencer in the kitchen. There was definitely something up. Why was Mum on the phone? Had someone died? Then Mum and Dad finally appeared with Chelsea trailing along behind.

'This had better be good,' Chelsea was complaining, 'I'm in the middle of something,' like *The Jeremy Kyle Show* was important or something.

And that's when it happened. The earthquake. Not a real one, this is England, but it was like an earthquake in the family and nothing would ever be the same again.

Spencer and Chelsea started fighting over the last Jammy Dodger when Mum said in a sort of quavery voice,

'I've just won the lottery.'

There was a moment's silence when everyone just stared at her. So she said it again.

'We've won the lottery.'

Then everyone was talking at once. 'What do you mean?' (me). 'It's only lunchtime, they haven't drawn it yet.' (Spencer). 'How much? Another tenner?' (Chelsea).

Mum waited until we'd all shut up then said,

'It's £3.7 million.'

Chelsea started screaming. Spencer got up and started to do a wild dance round the kitchen; Dad was laughing and hugging Mum. I made the tea. I put a lot of sugar in Mum's mug. After a while my face started to hurt because I couldn't stop smiling. When everyone had calmed down a bit, Spencer said, 'I still don't get it. The lottery hasn't even been drawn yet. Is this some sort of joke?'

Mum explained what had happened. When she got into Tesco, she'd filled in this week's lottery numbers and when she went to pay she found last week's ticket in her purse and realised that she'd never checked it because of the last minute panic about going on holiday. So she handed it to the cashier for him to put in the machine to check. He told her it was a winning ticket and that she needed to ring the number on the back of the ticket. Then the other cashier looked over his shoulder and said, 'Oh my God,' and they'd both stared at her with their mouths open. Then she realised that if she didn't get out of there quick there was going to be 'a scene'.

Mum hates 'scenes', so she grabbed the ticket and grabbed Chelsea, who was looking at the magazines and hadn't heard anything, and dashed out of the shop. She hadn't even done her shopping. Then when she got in the car she didn't want to say anything in case someone (she looked at Chelsea when she said this) started screaming and she didn't think she could cope with that in such a confined space, and she was worried that Dad might crash the car and she knew he likes to concentrate when he's got the caravan on the back, so she kept quiet until we got home.

'Where's the ticket?' asked Dad.

Mum put her hand down her blouse and rooted around in her bra. Mum has what Dad refers to as 'an ample bosom', which means she's got huge bazoomas and I could see Dad was getting worried because she could easily lose it in there. On the other hand, it was probably the safest place because no one was going to mess with Mum's bazoomas.

Mum found the ticket and Dad took it as if it was going to bite him. Spencer had sat back down and was munching on the biscuits again and Chelsea was just sitting there going 'Oh my God, Oh my God, Oh my God,' over and over again. Then she stopped and looked like a light had gone on in her head.

'Do you mean to say,' she said, 'that we've been million-aires for a whole week and all the time we were in

Weston-super-Mare we could have been living it up in the south of France, or somewhere?'

'Yes,' said Mum in an awed voice. 'Just think, we were millionaires all week and we didn't even know.'

'I can't believe it!' screeched Chelsea. 'We could have gone to Las Vegas or Miami, or Bermuda or . . . or . . . Florida . . . or . . .' She was desperately trying to think of all the places she wanted to go when Spencer chipped in and burst her bubble.

'Actually,' he told her, 'we couldn't have gone anywhere like that because none of us have got passports and there wouldn't have been time to arrange it.'

'I don't care,' said Chelsea. 'Anyhow, we could at least have gone somewhere nicer, like London, and stayed in a five star hotel and gone shopping all week and to loads of shows and stuff.'

'Yeah, like that's what the rest of us want to do!' said Spencer.

Everyone was quiet while we tried to take it in. For about three seconds – and then we all started screaming again. Mum took the ticket off Dad and tucked it back into her bra.

'Are we going to be on the telly?' said Chelsea, getting all excited again.

'God forbid,' said Mum. 'We'll have to tell our friends, I don't see how we're going to be able to keep it a secret, but I don't want a big fuss or anything,' she said, looking worried. 'It would look like we were showing off.'

It all got a bit weird after that. Dad said, lottery win or no lottery win, he had to take the caravan back to his brother. Mum said she'd go with him because she couldn't wait to see the look on Auntie Sheila's face when they told her.

So much for not showing off, I thought. But I couldn't blame her. Auntie Sheila is always rubbing it in that they've got more money than us. I was almost tempted to go with them just to see her face, but I wanted to go round to Lauren's; I'd promised her I'd go as soon as I got back from the holiday. Mum told me to invite them back for a drink and a bit of food later to celebrate.

'Nothing fancy, just family and close friends. We'll pick Grumps up on our way back.'

It was weird us all going our separate ways. I felt like something so enormous had happened that we should all stick together. I had butterflies in my stomach but I don't know if it was from excitement or nerves. Maybe it was just adrenalin. I ran all the way to Lauren's to try to get rid of the jittery feeling. Pam, Lauren's mum, opened the door.

'Mum's won the lottery,' I yelled. If it was a reaction I wanted, I certainly got one. Pam screamed which brought Lauren running down the stairs and her dad in from the garden. It took me a while to convince them it wasn't a joke and I had to explain that it was last week's ticket and we'd only just found out. There was some more screaming before Pam went off to ring Mum and congratulate her because Pam's been my mum's best friend since they were at school together.

'I can't believe it,' said Lauren. 'You are *so* lucky!'

I flopped down on the sofa, exhausted from all the screaming. Lauren sat down next to me.

'I can't believe it,' she said again. 'I'm so pleased. You're so lucky. Really, it's great. I'm so pleased for you.' I wondered why she had to say it so many times. I looked really hard to see if she meant it. I think her mouth was smiling at me but her eyes weren't sure.

'Whatever,' I said to lighten the moment. 'It's only money.'

'Yeah, it's only money,' she said back at me and pushed me over so I fell into the cushions. We ended up having a cushion fight and the moment passed. I mean, why wouldn't she be pleased?

Then Mum rang my mobile and said she'd got Grumps and they'd been to the supermarket, but not Tesco in case she was recognised, and we could all come back to the house and celebrate.

It was a funny sort of party. Uncle Ron turned up (apparently Auntie Sheila was suffering from a migraine, probably brought on by our good fortune, according to Mum). Grumps was looking happy for a change. Pam was helping Mum in the kitchen and Lauren's dad, Gary, was helping Dad with the barbecue. Spencer and Chelsea didn't invite anyone, but I had Lauren who's like part of the family anyway.

We were in the back garden messing around.

'Just think,' said Lauren, 'you'll be able to have one of those big trampolines . . . and a new bike. You could get some roller blades – though they're not much fun by yourself so you'll have to get me some as well.'

'I don't know what Mum and Dad are thinking of doing with the money but I don't think they're planning on spending it all on me,' I laughed. Lauren looked disappointed. 'But I'm sure I'll get some new things,' I said to cheer her up.

'If it was my mum I'd make her get me everything,' said Lauren. 'A new trampoline and a bike, a new phone, a laptop, a whole new wardrobe, an iPod, some real diamond earrings . . .' It was at that point that I wrestled her to the ground, sat on her and stuffed a burger bun in her mouth.

Later on, when the adults were a little bit drunk, Dad started to do his dancing. Grumps got up and joined him and said he'd show him a move or two. Lauren and I were giggling helplessly, imagining that Grumps was going to teach Dad to waltz or something. But after a quick whispered conversation with Chelsea, who was in charge of the music, she put on some hip hop and Grumps showed us his moves. At first everyone was speechless, then Mum started clapping and cheering and before long there was a dance off going on in the back garden. We all joined in – even Chelsea who normally wouldn't dance in front of all the grown ups. Lauren and I had to stop because we were laughing so much at our mums, who both looked like someone had put itching powder down their backs.

Grumps was definitely the winner, but then he got a bit ambitious and tried a head roll and Dad had to get him up. Gary wanted to know where he'd learnt to body pop and

Grumps said there'd been a class on down at the community hall. It was meant to get the lads from the estate to mix with the older generation so they could learn to respect each other.

Grumps said it was really good, because when you did hip hop you had to let everything 'hang loose' and you could do a lot of it just standing on the spot, so it turned out to be a great way for the oldies to stay fit, if they could stand the music. Grumps loved it and went along every week.

Eventually Dad took Grumps home because he'd fallen asleep in the chair and Lauren and her mum and dad left. We all did some half-hearted clearing up. No one wanted to go to bed. We were all too wound up to go to sleep and it seemed like too much of an ordinary thing to do. I fell asleep on the sofa at about one o'clock and Mum woke me up at three o'clock when everyone else went to bed. I'm still awake, though – I can't stop thinking about how great everything is going to be.

Sunday 29th August

This morning I woke up really early. It was sort of light out-side, but only just. Chelsea, despite her claim that she wasn't going to sleep last night, was snoring loudly above me. I decided to go downstairs and see what the television had to offer at the crack of dawn.

Mum was sitting at the kitchen table with her hands round a cup of coffee.

'Couldn't you sleep, either?' she said, pulling the chair out next to her. 'I had to wear my bra to bed to keep the ticket safe. It was really uncomfortable.'

'Chelsea's snoring,' I explained, sitting down.

Mum gave me a hug with one arm. 'At least I've stopped shaking now.' She held out her hand to prove it to me. It started wobbling. We laughed. 'It's the shock,' she said.

'People will think you've been drinking,' I told her.

'They can think what they like. I don't care; I'm a million-airess.'

We giggled like Lauren and I do sometimes, sitting at the back in French. It was nice. Not that Mum isn't usually happy, because she is, but this was exciting, and it was fun being up so early when everyone else was asleep.

'What's going to happen?' I said. 'I mean, what happens now?'

'Well, Dad and I are going to London on Wednesday to collect the prize money. I think we'll come straight back afterwards. We did think about spending the night there in a posh hotel and seeing a show, but you know what your Dad's like with hotels.' I didn't, but I kept quiet because I didn't want to interrupt. Besides, I could imagine that he'd be really uncomfortable with people running round, carrying his luggage for him and he'd be worrying about how much he'd have to tip them.

'Besides, you've all got your first day back at school so it won't seem right not to be here and I don't want to have to ask Grumps to come and stay over; you know what he's like.'

This time I did know what she meant. Grumps isn't the best childminder in the world. Last time he looked after us Mum told him to give us fishfingers and chips for tea because it was easy. Grumps tried to make the chips in an old deep fat fryer he found at the back of a cupboard and it caught alight and nearly burnt the house down. Spencer had to explain to him about oven chips and in the end we cooked it ourselves, once the smoke had cleared out of the kitchen.

43

'I think the best thing is to try and keep everything as normal as possible until we've had time to think.'

'Can't we come to London with you?'

'Do you want to? It'll probably be really boring and you'd miss the first day back at school. Besides, I don't think we can afford train fares for all of us . . .' Then she realised what she'd said and we were off laughing again.

'What's so funny?' Chelsea appeared in the doorway, looking sleepy and crumpled but perfectly happy. 'What time is it?'

'It's half past five,' said Mum. 'I haven't seen you up so early since Christmas morning when you were four.'

Chelsea groaned. 'Why does it have to be Sunday today. The shops don't open until ten o'clock! We are going to have the most amazing shopping trip ever.'

Mum looked uncertain. 'It might have to wait until we've actually got the money. I wouldn't be comfortable spending money until it's in my bank account . . .'

Chelsea sat down opposite Mum. 'Okay, fine,' she said, taking a biscuit out of the tin and nibbling on it. This new Chelsea was making me nervous. No way was it fine with her. Why did she look so relaxed? I should have known better.

'So, Mum. What are you going to wear when you go up to London? You'll need to look smart . . . you'll have to knock them out with your outfit.'

Chelsea continued to nibble, eyeing Mum over her biscuit. 'Have you still got that flowery dress you wore to

Uncle Ron's wedding? It was only ten years ago; it should still fit you. There's always the old reliable black skirt and white blouse but then you might be mistaken for one of the waitresses handing out champagne. I've heard they put on quite a party at Camelot . . .'

She'd said enough. Mum looked totally panicked. I have to admire Chelsea at moments like this. She certainly knows exactly the right buttons to push.

'Maybe it can't do any harm to go and have a look in Marks and Spencer's,' Mum said.

I went back to bed. If we were going shopping I'd need all the strength I could get. I finally drifted off to sleep to the sound of Chelsea singing as she took a long soak in the bath.

We all set off together for the shopping trip. There was a bit of a panic before we left the house because Mum didn't want to take the ticket with her. She said she'd be too worried about losing it and besides she might be trying clothes on. Everyone started suggesting the best place to put it. Spencer tried to stick it onto the fridge with a fridge magnet but Chelsea told him not to be so stupid. Word about our win was bound to be all over the estate and someone might break in and nick it.

Mum started to panic even though Spencer tried to persuade her that this wasn't going to happen and, even if it did, they'd never be able to claim the money because the cashier in Tesco was witness to the fact that it was her ticket. In the end she hid it in the teabag tin, underneath the teabags.

After we'd parked the car, Dad and Spencer sloped off, saying they had to go and check something out in the computer shop.

I soon wished I'd stayed at home. Clothes shopping isn't exactly my favourite thing. Every morning (except the weekends, obviously) I'm actually thankful for my school uniform; weird, I know, but at least it means I don't have to think about what I'm going to wear.

Eventually we stopped for lunch. Chelsea tried to drag Mum into a hyper-trendy restaurant by the river, but Mum put her foot down when she saw the menu by the door.

'Twenty-two pounds for a plate of fish and chips!' Mum was seriously outraged.

'But Mum, it doesn't matter any more,' explained Chelsea patiently. 'You can afford it now – you're a millionaire, remember?'

'I don't care,' said Mum. 'I wouldn't pay that much even if I was a *billionaire*. It's not right.'

I could see Chelsea was seriously disappointed, but she knew when she was beaten. We still had a nice lunch at our usual café, only this time we could have what we wanted and didn't have to go for the special offers, though I noticed Mum did anyway.

Dad and Spencer joined us for lunch but then disappeared again – Spencer mumbling something about the Games Workshop.

It wasn't until Mum and Chelsea were collecting all their

bags together that they even noticed me and my lack of shopping.

'Charlotte! Haven't you got anything?' said Mum, looking concerned. 'Didn't you see any nice clothes you wanted?'

The truth is that I hadn't. I had looked while Mum and Chelsea were busy but I couldn't find anything. I was about to say, 'I don't know *what* to get,' but I could see from the glint in Chelsea's eye that she was planning a massive makeover for me.

'Ooh, there is something I really want,' I said quickly before she could drag me into Top Shop. 'I really need a new notebook and some pens and stuff, for school on Wednesday. And maybe a new school bag,' I added, improvising madly, 'and I wouldn't mind going to the bookshop.'

Chelsea heaved a huge sigh. 'Can't you just give her some money, Mum, and then she can go and get all her boring stuff while we finish our proper shopping?'

In the end, Mum agreed and we went to the cash machine. I could tell Mum was nervous getting so much money out. She gave me a hundred pounds! Then she changed her mind and took thirty away. I didn't complain because I would have been a bit frightened walking around on my own with that much money.

I soon wished I hadn't been so pathetic though, because once I started spending, I couldn't stop, and the money was soon all gone.

I spent about an hour in Paperchase drooling over all the lovely notebooks (not literally, obviously, or they would have thrown me out for ruining their stock). In the end, I chose a lovely one covered in birds and leaves. I bought a pen with *Charlotte* printed on it and a pencil case. I found a new bag for school then spent the rest of the time (and the money) in the bookshop. I ended up with seven books and I was glad I'd bought a new bag because I knew what Chelsea would say if she saw I'd spent most of my money on books. This way I could hide them in my bag and hope she didn't ask me what I'd bought.

Not that I needed to worry on that score. When I got back to the car the others were already there, trying to fit all the bags into the boot. Mum had obviously overcome her worry about spending the money before she'd picked up the cheque. I'd never seen so many bags! Chelsea was on a shopping high and was going on about all the stuff her and Mum had bought even though nobody was listening.

On the way home I wondered where I was going to put all my new books. We only had a tiny bookcase in our bedroom and it was already full. I really wish I could have a big bookcase full of lovely books. And a quiet corner to read them in. We were driving down a street with big old houses and I saw a 'for sale' sign.

'Mum? Are we going to buy a new house?' I couldn't believe I hadn't thought about this before now, but I couldn't remember anyone saying anything about it. They must have talked about it last night after I'd fallen asleep, because Chelsea said,

'Well, duh. Of course we are. Why would we stay in our

48

poxy house when we could be living in luxury? I wonder about you sometimes, I really do. Mum, are you sure you didn't adopt Charlotte? Or bring the wrong baby home from the hospital?'

'It was you that got mixed up at the hospital, not me,' I retorted.

'Enough,' said Mum. I shut up, because I wanted to know the answer to my question.

'We'll have to move, because it wouldn't be fair to stay in a council house when there are people out there who really need them.'

'We could buy someone else a house and stay in ours if it makes you feel better,' said Spencer.

Chelsea hit him and I said, 'It's all right for you, you've got your own bedroom. If it was you sharing with Chelsea, you'd be down the estate agent's first thing tomorrow, trust me.'

'The important thing is not to do anything too hasty,' said Mum. 'Let's just wait and see, shall we?'

Now we're back I'm sitting on my bunk, keeping out of the way while Chelsea examines all her new clothes. Sixth Formers are allowed to wear their own clothes to school. Chelsea was just holding up a new top and admiring herself in the mirror.

She opened a drawer and started pulling things out to make way for her new stuff. First to go was her old school uniform and she threw it at me, saying, 'There you go. It's all yours. You might grow into it one day, you never know.'

'What, you mean like one day – when I'm *pregnant*,' I said. Chelsea's not really fat but every time she teases me about my height, I tease her about her weight.

I can't wait until I've got my own room and won't have to climb over piles of clothes any more or listen to Chelsea scream and shout when she can't find a clean pair of knickers. I shall be blissfully unaware, in my own wing with any luck.

Monday 30th August

Today was frighteningly normal, considering that we're now millionaires. Chelsea wanted to go shopping again, but Mum said half the shops would be shut on a bank holiday so Chelsea started to look on the internet for a new house. Then a fight broke out because Spencer needed the internet as well and we've only got the one computer. Dad broke it up and told Chelsea to let Spencer use it because he needed it more.

'What could be more important than finding us a new house?' shouted Chelsea.

'Finding me a new school,' Spencer shouted back.

It turned out that Spencer had decided he wanted to go to a new school, and now Mum and Dad could afford for him to go to a private school they'd agreed that he could have a look at some.

'That's not fair,' shouted Chelsea. 'What if I want to go to a new school as well? Can't I go to one of those posh boarding schools?'

I thought that was a brilliant idea and held my breath, hoping that Mum would agree. 'Nobody is going to boarding school,' said Mum firmly. 'I didn't have children just to let someone else bring them up.'

I don't think she's thought that one through. I'd be happy if Chelsea went to boarding school. The only boarding school I'd want to go to is Hogwarts and that's never going to happen.

In the end, Chelsea stomped off to our room and Dad and Spencer looked up schools in our area. I could hear Spencer telling Dad that perhaps he should think about sending Chelsea to Brat Camp now we could afford it.

'You might be right, son,' Dad muttered back.

I went round to Lauren's house.

Tuesday 31st August

Mum, Dad and Spencer went out this morning. They've managed to get an emergency interview with the headmaster of the school that Spencer wants to go to. Spencer was dead nervous in case he had to sit an exam, but Dad said it was unlikely and his reports from Avon Comp should be enough to get him a place.

I was just settling down with a good book when Chelsea wandered into the room. She was all dressed up and looked amazing. I wondered if she'd finally got a date with Josh and decided she must have, because she kept looking out of the window like she was expecting someone.

She was re-doing her mascara in the hall mirror when the doorbell rang. I peeped through the window to get a look at her hot date and nearly died from shock. There were loads of people on the doorstep! There was even a bloke

53

with a television camera balanced on his shoulder. I ducked down and crawled across the room, then peered round the door. Chelsea had flung the door open and was standing on the doorstep talking to them! I was nearly blinded by the flashes going off on their cameras but Chelsea stood there striking a pose. They all started firing questions at her and she was laughing and chatting away like she was used to having the paparazzi camped on her doorstep.

Her moment of fame didn't last long though. As soon as the reporters discovered that it wasn't her who had bought the lottery ticket, the flashes stopped going off and the man with the TV camera wearily lowered it off his shoulder. 'So when will your mum be back then?' said one of them, looking at his watch.

'Any minute now,' said Chelsea. 'Maybe you could do an article on what it's like to be the daughter of a lottery winner,' she added desperately. None of them looked convinced that that would be a good idea. One of the reporters' phones went off and he peeled away. The others were eyeing him nervously and I could tell that they were all worried that he'd got a bigger, better story and they were wondering whether or not to follow him. I was worried that Chelsea would get so desperate to keep them there that she'd end up doing something stupid, like strip off or something.

Thankfully, at that moment, our car pulled up and Mum and Dad got out, so all the reporters dashed over there and the flashes started going off again. Chelsea pouted. Then Spencer slunk up the garden path, so I followed him into the kitchen to find out how it went at the school. He was really excited and said it was awesome and the science labs were excellent and the headmaster had said he could start there at the beginning of term. Spencer gets longer holidays now so he doesn't have to go back to school tomorrow like me. He didn't rub it in though.

Later we all watched the local news and Mum and Dad were on it. Mum looked a bit shocked, which I guess anyone would if they'd just got out of their car and found themselves in the limelight. Chelsea was furious, because all the bits she'd done before Mum and Dad got back had been cut and she wasn't on it at all.

'I wonder how they found out,' said Mum. 'I suppose the people at Tesco must have tipped them off.'

I didn't point out that they couldn't have known where we lived or that Chelsea was even more tarted up than usual.

Wednesday 1st September

It was great to be back at school. As usual, Lauren called for me on her way past and then we met up with Karly and Tiffany. I was a bit nervous because I didn't know if news about our win had got round the school. It wasn't too bad though. Everyone was over-excited anyway about meeting up with all their friends again.

Chelsea caused a bit of a scene this morning when she realised she wasn't going up to London with Mum and Dad, but then she calmed down because she didn't want to miss her first day back and all the fuss our win would cause at school. I could tell she was dying to tell Sophie and Amber about it.

Some of the other girls in my form were standing about having a laugh at the newbies in Year 7. Their uniforms were too big and too tidy and they either looked really nervous or overly cocky. I was trying not to get hung up on the fact that most of them were taller than me.

Occasionally someone would come up to me and say, 'Is it true your mum won the lottery?' and Lauren would tell them to go away.

Of course, Karly and Tiffany wanted all the news and I didn't mind telling *them* about it. I had been terrified that they might be funny with me but I needn't have worried. They were my friends and it was so good to be back. Every one was talking at once and saying what they'd buy and which clothes shops they'd go in and where they'd go on holiday. I was about to say that it was my mum who'd won the money and it wasn't as if I suddenly had millions to personally dispose of, but I kept quiet in the end because they were having so much fun.

'I'd buy shoes,' said Karly. 'Thousands of them, and a whole room to keep them in.'

Tiffany said she'd get a horse. 'A proper one, one of those Arabian stallions, not a pony or anything. Please say you'll get a horse, Charlotte, and then I can come and ride it.' I didn't like to point out that a horse in the middle of Bristol just wasn't going to work. It got me thinking though. I'd always wished I could have a pet but Mum always said the house was too small. I brought the school hamster home for the holidays once to try and convince her that no house was too small for a hamster, but it kept everyone awake all night going round on its wheel; even when we shut it in the kitchen, so I guess she was right.

Some of the boys took to calling me Charlottery for a bit, but it wasn't that funny so it soon wore off. I wondered what was happening in the Sixth Form. I was sure that Chelsea would be milking the attention.

The only lesson I don't have with Lauren this year is maths, because she's in the top set and I'm in the bottom set. However hard I try I'm just hopeless at it. Not like Spencer, who seems to have been born with a calculator embedded in his brain.

Everything was so reassuringly normal. We had the same form tutor as last year, Mr Lawson. The school had decided that we'd stick with the same form tutor all through lower school, so we'd get him next year as well, which was fine because he was nice and funny but not in a sad 'I'm trying to get down with the kids' way. I feel sorry for the other form though, because they're stuck with old Beecham for three years and she's horrible. She's definitely had a sense of humour bypass. She takes us for RE and I'm sure she goes out of her way to make it as boring as humanly possible.

The best thing about being back at school is that I don't get the strange feeling I've had at home recently; that everything isn't quite real. I've stopped waking up in the morning and getting a shock when I remember that we're rich now. We still have to get ready for school and do all the normal things that we've always done but somehow, at home, it feels like we're in limbo. I suppose, when we've found a new house and moved in, everything will feel more normal.

No one could believe it this evening when Dad said he

was going to keep his job as a delivery van driver. Only Grumps agreed with him that it was a good idea.

'I like my job,' explained Dad. 'It gets me out and about and I like meeting people. I've got a lot of regular customers and they'd miss me if I stopped.'

Mum said her ladies were going to have to miss her because she wasn't going out cleaning houses any more. Except for Miss Evans. She'd keep Miss Evans on, because she reckoned that sometimes she was the only person Miss Evans spoke to all week and she didn't like to abandon her, though she would feel guilty about taking her money because she didn't think Miss Evans had a lot.

Thursday 9th September

Chelsea's taken it upon herself to find us a new house. She's gone completely mental. She spends all night on the internet looking at property sites and selecting new houses to go and look at. The only problem is, she needs Mum and Dad to make the appointment with the estate agents to go and view them. When her wheedling doesn't work and they refuse to go and look at the latest 'amazing' house, she goes off in an enormous sulk.

Mum and Dad finally agreed to go and look at one house she's found. I think they're only going to keep her quiet. Also, Chelsea's so enthusiastic about it all that it's hard not to get caught up in her excitement and Mum always tries to encourage us in our hobbies. Like when I was really into my project on Amy Johnson, she got Dad to drive us all the way to the aviation museum so I could see the kind of plane Amy would have flown. I think Dad enjoyed it more than me. He got quite excited and Mum had to drag him away before we all got locked in there for the night.

So on Saturday we're all going to look at the house that Chelsea has decided is going to be our new home.

Saturday 11th September

It was weird looking round someone else's home and trying to imagine living there. I know I did it when I went with Mum to the Bings', but that was just pretend whereas this is real.

Not that anyone except Chelsea could see themselves living in that house.

It was massive and very, very modern. It seemed to have more windows than walls, and it even had a swimming pool. Chelsea says we have to have a swimming pool now we're millionaires.

Dad said that the kitchen looked like an operating theatre and he wasn't sure he wanted to eat anything that came out of a place that reminded him of major surgical procedures.

I could see Mum eyeing the two storey windows and all

the polished surfaces. I bet she was wondering what the best cleaning products would be to use on them and worrying about how she'd keep them clean.

Chelsea loved every minute of it. I could see that she was imagining all the parties she could have there and how all her friends would be impressed. The pool certainly put Sophie Jacobs' hot-tub in the shade.

I wish Spencer had come with us. We could have had a good laugh at all the pictures and sculptures. They were everywhere and were all nude people in some pretty contorted positions. I was dying to impersonate some of them but only Spencer would have found it funny. He didn't come because he said he had too much homework. The new school have sent him work to do so that he's not behind with it when he starts there. I can't imagine Spencer being behind with his work. Personally, I think it was just an excuse. I honestly believe he doesn't care where we live.

The estate agent was working really hard to try and sell the house to Mum and Dad but I think he knew that they didn't really like it. Chelsea tried to get me on her side by telling me that I could have the best bedroom. Obviously, I wasn't taken in. I knew that the moment we moved in she'd nab that room because it had a roll top bath in the en suite and a walk-in wardrobe.

It *was* an amazing house, but I couldn't really see us living there. It wasn't what you'd describe as cosy or homely.

Now we'll have to put up with Chelsea raving about it

for the next two weeks until Mum and Dad eventually buy it just to keep her quiet. Chelsea has that effect on people.

When we got home, it was kind of sad. Going to see such a lovely house made our three-bedroom council house feel even more pokey and shabby than usual, even though it's not that bad really, and it does feel like home. Although I really want to move because I want my own room, I'll be sorry to leave this house. Also, Lauren only lives down the road and we can see each other whenever we want. I wonder if I can persuade Mum and Dad to buy a house not far from here.

Monday 13th September

We got our diary homework back today from Mrs Harper. She'd put 'very good' on mine. I didn't think it was that good. I'd only written a load of rubbish about Weston-super-Mare. I didn't put all the stuff about Chelsea going off or the cave guide being a troll, like I put in my real diary. I wonder what comment Mrs Harper would make about this one.

Spencer started at his new school today. He did look funny in his smart new uniform. I felt nervous for him but he seemed to be totally unfazed, though he did check his bag about six times to make sure he had everything.

He will have to go on the bus, but Dad said he would give him a lift there for the first few days, just until he's settled in. I wonder what they'll make of Dad's delivery van pulling up in front of such a posh school. I mentioned this to Spencer, but he said it wasn't a problem and that the school wasn't *that* posh really. It was just a normal school, except you had to pay to go to it and have really good grades. It wasn't like one of those boys' public schools or really expensive boarding schools. I felt better after that. I hoped that, if all the people there were clever, then Spencer wouldn't get picked on for being brainy.

When Lauren and I got to school this morning there was a bit of a buzz in the playground. There were groups of people hanging around, chatting, and when we walked by some of them gave me funny looks. I immediately felt paranoid and wondered what I could have done. Apart from the lottery win, which people still occasionally asked me about, I couldn't think of anything. We found Karly and Tiffany and asked them what was going on.

'There's just been a stand-off between Sophie and Chelsea at the school gates,' said Karly.

I groaned. I thought Chelsea had vowed never to speak to Sophie again, although I didn't really know what had been happening because the Sixth Form block is so separate from the rest of the school.

Apparently, Chelsea had been describing, in a very loud voice, the house we had been to see and how, when we'd moved in, she was going to have the most amazing pool party. Sophie had been passing and said, 'You can take the girl out of the council estate, but you can't take the council estate out of the girl.'

Chelsea had come back really quickly with, 'And you'll never take the Nob out of Snob.' According to Karly, who had seen it all, this had got a huge laugh from everyone. Even Josh had laughed and that had really wound Sophie up and she'd hit him with her bag and stormed off. Josh had just shrugged and winked at Chelsea.

I knew it wouldn't take much to spark off a war between the Ratcliffe estate kids and the rich kids. And if that happened, where would Chelsea and I stand? We might be rich now, but we weren't in with that crowd – all our friends were Ratcliffe estate and they all tended to stick together. When we moved, would they think we weren't one of them any more? I was so upset I was shaking. But I knew I was being silly. Lauren wasn't suddenly going to stop being friends with me just because we'd moved house!

Tuesday 21st September

There are definite tensions at school. Chelsea and Sophie are now openly hostile towards each other. Sophie must have made it up with Josh though, because I saw them snogging at the bus stop. It's not just the Sixth Formers either. I heard two Year 7s talking about it at break time, and Chelsea is going round with the estate girls now, the really hard ones that live in the flats and that she's always avoided until now. I think the teachers have got wind of it though, because they've started patrolling the playground and corridors at break and lunchtimes so I don't think anything will happen.

Lauren, Karly, Tiffany and I have all decided to rise above it and not get involved.

Lauren and I spent the lunch hour trying to decide which after-school club to join. I fancied the book club but Lauren hated that idea. She fancied the choir because the music teacher is male and good-looking. I had to remind her that I'm tone deaf and I'd be thrown out for singing out of tune. In the end, we decided not to bother because there wasn't anything we both wanted to do. As we were leaving, I saw Alec putting his name down for the War Hammer club. I said hi to him because he looked so lost without Spencer. Alec's really brainy too and they've always stuck together. I felt bad for him being on his own now. I wonder if Spencer will still meet up with him on Saturdays to go to the Games Workshop or whether he'll be too busy with all his new friends.

Saturday 2nd October

Today, at breakfast, Mum and Dad announced that we were going to view another house. It's quite unusual for us all to be having breakfast at the same time on a Saturday morning. Normally Chelsea would still be in bed, but Mum and Dad had agreed to raise her allowance, so she was planning to go on a spending spree. They've raised my pocket money too. Mum said that when I want to start buying my own clothes I can have an allowance as well but at the moment I don't really need one. I'm still happy to go shopping with Mum if I need anything as I'm not that interested in clothes and stuff.

Chelsea said she wasn't coming to see the house because she was too busy.

'Why do we need to look at more houses?' she said. 'I thought we were going to buy the one with the pool, so what's the point?'

'We never said we were going to buy that house, Chelsea,' said Dad.

Chelsea flicked her hair back and took a deep breath in. It was a sure sign that she was about to list (again) all the reasons why we had to buy the house she'd chosen.

Mum, who had been clearing away the breakfast, got in first. 'We're all going and that's an end to it. Half an hour everyone,' she said, clapping her hands, because only Spencer was actually dressed.

Chelsea let her indrawn breath out in a big huff, but she knew there was no point in arguing with Mum when she used that no-nonsense voice. There was always the possibility that her newly inflated allowance would be cut back to its original size if she refused.

I was halfway up the stairs when Chelsea barged past me and headed for the bathroom, locking the door behind her. Typical. So I'm waiting for her to come out. I hope the house we finally buy has more than one bathroom. Most houses do these days, I've discovered. Ever since I found out we were going to move, I've started watching property programmes on the television. Mostly they're people who want to move and they get the presenters to find them a house. I wonder why Chelsea has never thought of applying to take part in one of the shows, seeing as she's so fond of the limelight.

And that is the main difference between us. Chelsea seems to live her life on full power. She's either mega happy or super stroppy. Everything is a drama and she has to be centre stage. I, on the other hand, am the opposite. Like Mum, I don't like a scene. I'd be quite happy if nothing dramatic ever happened to me. I like everything to be calm and predictable. Not in a boring way, just in a reassuring way.

We all piled into the car and Dad drove to the estate agent's to pick up the keys. This meant that I couldn't really judge how far this house was going to be from ours. I didn't want to look at a house that was miles away from Lauren's.

We drove up some pretty steep hills and I reckoned we were in the Clifton area of town. I relaxed a bit because that was only a short bus ride from our estate.

Dad slowed down and finally turned into a driveway between two big stone pillars with round stone balls on top. The pillar on the left said *HILL* and the one on the right said *HOUSE*.

I was craning to get a look at the house but the drive was bordered by great big shrubs. Then we drove round a bend and the house came into view.

Chelsea gasped. 'You are kidding, right?'

Spencer looked up from his DS to see what all the fuss was about. 'Cool,' he said, and I had to agree with him.

Chelsea was less than impressed. 'Are we changing our surname to Addams?' she sounded seriously outraged. 'I'm not going in there. There're probably bats in the belfry and God knows what else.'

It did look a bit Addams Family. There was even a turret on one corner with a conical roof. The large oak front door was impressive and the porch reminded me of the entrance to a church. I couldn't wait to get inside.

'Victorian Gothic,' said Mum. 'Isn't it gorgeous?'

'If you're a goth, maybe,' said Chelsea, 'or a vampire. I'm waiting here, so don't be long.' She produced a nail file from her bag and started on her nails. 'Hill House, my arse,' she muttered. 'More like Hell House.'

'Come on,' said Dad. 'You'll love it when you see the inside.'

'God, this is such a waste of time. I could be out shopping,' she said, but she put the nail file away and followed us to the front door. Dad got the keys out and grinned at Mum. Then he ceremoniously flung open the door.

The hallway was probably as big as our sitting room at home. It had a patterned, tiled floor and a wide staircase leading up to a half landing, where there was a stained-glass window. The sun chose that moment to come out and the hallway was suddenly bathed in a rainbow of colours. I half expected dramatic music to ring throughout the house.

'Well, go on then,' said Dad. 'Go and explore.'

Chelsea seemed reluctant to move any further into the house. 'Does anyone actually live here?' she asked.

'No,' said Dad. 'The house belonged to a very old man who lived here all his life. It's an absolute gem. Totally unspoilt.'

73

'You mean totally *unmodernised*,' muttered Chelsea. 'What a nightmare!'

I tried to ignore her mutterings because I was enjoying a nice, warm, cosy feeling that had come over me. I could see us living in this house and I hadn't even gone further than the hallway.

'It's got four bedrooms on the next floor,' said Dad, 'and two more in the attics, so no fighting over them.'

Mum went back out to the car and started rummaging in the boot and Dad disappeared through a door at the back of the hall.

'They must be mad,' said Chelsea. 'We're never buying this house.'

I didn't like to point out to her that it was Mum and Dad who would be choosing a house and not her. At least I hoped so. Chelsea has an uncanny ability of always getting her own way.

Spencer and I spent the next hour exploring. The house was big, but not too big. We started in the attics, which Spencer got quite excited about. They were just two big rooms but, as Spencer had always slept in the box room at home, I could empathise with his dream of having space, at last, to put out all his War Hammer stuff. When Dad had said attics, I'd imagined pokey, dusty rooms with sloping ceilings but this wasn't the case. Each room had a large, arch-shaped window that looked out over the garden in the back one and the street in the front one. I could see that Spencer favoured the back room and was already mentally moving in. I wasn't going to commit myself to a room; I didn't want to get too excited just to be disappointed when we moved into the glass monstrosity of Chelsea's choosing.

'Do you want that room in the front, opposite mine?' said Spencer.

It was sweet of him, but I wasn't sure I wanted to be that close to Spencer's piles of smelly socks and the late night explosions from his computer games.

'Let's look at the other rooms first,' I said, leading the way downstairs.

I was suddenly very excited but also anxious. I'd dreamt of having my own room for so long and now that it was going to happen I was worried I'd be disappointed with the choice. Mind you, not that I was likely to get much of a choice. Even if we did buy this house, Mum and Dad would get the master bedroom in the turret and then Chelsea would pick the next best. But at least that would leave me with a choice of the remaining rooms.

Back on the landing I paused. There was an archway that led to the two back bedrooms. What if they were awful? What if they were dark and had ghastly wallpaper?

'Come on,' said Spencer, charging off down the corridor. First on the right was a door which turned out to be the bathroom. It wasn't exactly modern but there was a big shower head over the bath. I liked it, but Spencer wasn't going to linger in a bathroom so we shut the door and carried on to the next door on the left.

'Whoa,' said Spencer. 'This must be Morticia's boudoir.'

I followed him in. The room was dark, because there was a large tree outside the window blocking most of the light. The walls were covered with the most hideous green and purple wallpaper and there was a huge wardrobe on the back wall, just like the Bings'. I suppressed a shudder. You won't catch me climbing in there; you'd be more likely to come out in hell than Narnia.

The room had the ability (like one of the Dementors in *Harry Potter*) of sucking all the hope and joy out of a person. Spencer shivered. He obviously felt it too, so I knew I wasn't being weird.

'Let's find the other one,' he said cheerfully, for my benefit, though I could tell, like me, he was dying to get out of there.

At the end of the corridor there was a smaller archway and a couple of steps down.

'Looks like we're in the servants' quarters,' Spencer commented.

'I thought servants always slept in the attic,' I said, trying to keep the worry out of my voice. Not that it mattered, I kept telling myself. I'd sleep in the cupboard under the stairs if it meant I had it to myself. And besides, if the next one was as bad as the last, I'd sleep in the other attic room.

Spencer stopped at the door, as if he already thought of it as my room, and let me go in first. I stepped inside and looked around.

'Oh well,' said Spencer, peering over my shoulder, 'looks like you'll be in the attic with me, then.'

I hadn't realised I'd been holding my breath until it came out in a big sigh.

'What do mean? It's absolutely perfect,' I eventually managed to say.

I was still taking it all in. I suppose Spencer thought I wouldn't like it because it was smaller than all the other rooms. But that was one of the things I liked about it. It had a bay window overlooking the garden which let in plenty of light, and the thing that I couldn't take my eyes off was the wall between the bay window and the little window at the back of the room. The whole wall was covered with book-shelves. Floor to ceiling bookshelves. I mentally put all my books in place and reckoned they'd take up about two of the twelve shelves.

On the opposite wall was a tiny fireplace. There was wallpaper on that wall but it was lovely. I could definitely live with it. It was pale blue with tiny sprigs of flowers. Maybe not what I would have chosen myself, but it was growing on me already. Mind you, I think that if there had been a hole in the roof I would have told myself I could live with it, because I had fallen head over heels in love.

'Whatever floats your boat,' said Spencer. I was just grateful that he hadn't fallen in love with it too. I was pretty sure that Chelsea wouldn't want it.

I ran my hand over the polished wood of the shelves. It was funny really. Only the other day I'd been wishing I had somewhere to put all my books.

And that's when it hit me. Because a bookcase wasn't the

only thing I'd wished for. In fact, thinking about it, everything I'd wished for, when Spencer found the card from the arcade machine under my pillow at the caravan site, had so far come true.

'Spencer?' I said. 'Do you remember on holiday when I made those wishes? I wished we could afford a better holiday, which we definitely can now, even if we haven't been on one yet. And I wished I had a room of my own and that thing about you not being picked on at school for being the cleverest. Well, now you aren't because you're at a new school, aren't you? And now here are the bookshelves I wished for on the way back from our first shopping trip.'

Spencer was looking at me and his eyes were huge. 'Oh my God! Gypsy Ginny is making your dreams come true!'

And then he grinned and made spooky music noises and fell over laughing.

'Oh, Charlotte, please wish away all my spots and please wish that Emma Lilywhite lurves me!' he said.

I kicked him. Not hard, just enough to make me feel better. I could feel myself blushing. I really must get a grip. If Spencer tells Chelsea what I'd said about the wishes, I might as well be dead.

'Who's Emma Lilywhite?' I demanded.

Now it was his turn to blush. 'No one,' he mumbled. No doubt she was the hottest girl at his new school. I looked at Spencer with his tufty hair and glasses and pimples and knew that no girl was going to fancy him for a few years yet. I wish someone would see past the geeky exterior and appreciate him for what he is.

God, I'm doing it again! Making random wishes! I really ought to be more careful. No, get a grip – there is no way my wishes are being granted.

Anyway, Spencer and I were staring at each other and there was an unspoken agreement that he wouldn't mention my crazy wish thing if I never mentioned Emma Lilywhite again.

'Let's go and find the others. We haven't seen the kitchen yet,' he said.

I didn't want to leave 'my' room and I knew I would die if Mum and Dad didn't buy this house. As if Spencer could read my mind he said, 'All we have to do is convince Mum and Dad to buy this house.'

'Chelsea will go mad,' I said. 'Seriously mental.'

Just then, the door to the back of the house opened and Chelsea came out into the hall.

'Don't say we like it until I've eaten my lunch,' whispered Spencer. 'I don't want indigestion.'

'Lunch is ready, children,' Chelsea called, looking scorn-fully up the stairs at us.

'Oooh, hark at Nursey!' said Spencer, swinging his leg over the polished banister and sliding down the last bit. Luckily he managed to stop himself before he hit the ornately carved post at the bottom.

We followed Chelsea down a stone passage into the kitchen. It wasn't too bad as kitchens go. Whoever had cleared the house had left behind the biggest pieces of furniture. One of the walls was taken up with a built-in dresser and there was a huge Aga in the old fireplace. I could see why Mum was smiling. The big pine table in the middle had also been left, although there were no chairs to sit on. Someone, probably Dad, had found an assortment of packing cases and crates which he had overturned so we didn't have to stand up to eat our lunch. Spencer and I were still in a silly, giggly mood which just seemed to annoy Chelsea.

'God, look at this place,' she said, somehow encompassing not only the kitchen but the whole house in her disapproving look. 'What's the point in buying a place where you'd have to rip everything out and start again? At least with the other house we can move straight in and won't have to do anything.'

'Which bedroom did you like?' I asked her to get her off the subject of the other house.

'God, I don't know, I didn't look. What's the point? We won't be buying this heap.'

Mum brought out a flask full of coffee and some mugs. She was bustling round the kitchen like she already owned it.

We munched our sandwiches in silence for a bit. Chelsea had found the estate agent's details about the house and was rifling through them.

'For heaven's sake,' she said, pointing at the top of the first page. 'This house isn't even worth a million quid! What's the point of being a millionaire if you can't live in a million pound property?'

It was only five thousand pounds short of a million, I

noticed, reading the price upside down. But then the house she was so keen on was selling for £2.2 million.

That started Dad off on an explanation about 'capital' and 'interest rates' which is when I lost interest. I picked up my tuna sandwich and wandered outside. The sun was still out so I sat down on the step outside the kitchen door. There was a sort of cobbled courtyard with a load of outbuildings that I guessed were for storing coal in the old days. One of them might even be an outside loo. I smiled to myself when I thought what Chelsea would have to say about that.

One of the doors was rotten at the bottom and there was a hole. As I nibbled my sandwich, thinking that I wasn't really that hungry, I caught a movement behind the rotting door. I froze. I was tempted to scream because I was convinced it was a rat, but I didn't want to draw attention to it. It would only give Chelsea more ammunition in her fight against the house. Then a head popped out of the hole, followed by a big furry body, and I had to laugh because I was so relieved. It was only a cat. It sat down carefully on the cobbles and curled its tail neatly round its feet. We observed each other. It was a lovely cat – white and long-haired with green eyes. The tip of its tail and ears were ginger.

Very carefully, I extended my hand and made kissing noises. The cat blinked, then trotted up to me. It stopped about half a metre away and I could see it was poised to run if I turned out to be scary. But it lifted its nose up and I realised it had caught the smell of my tuna sandwich. I peeled the bread apart and threw it a bit of fish. I threw it another piece, a bit closer this time, and after the third piece the cat was happily polishing off the rest of the sandwich out of my hand. When it was satisfied that it had licked every scrap of tuna and butter off the slices of bread, it had a quick wash then rubbed itself against my legs. I decided it was too dainty to be a male cat and I wondered what she was called and which house she lived in. I was busy tickling her under her chin when there was an eruption from the kitchen behind me – 'Nooo! NO!' followed by a kind of animal screech. The cat was gone before I'd jumped up and stuck my head in the door to see what was going on. I just caught a glimpse of Chelsea as she stormed out through the opposite door.

When I looked at Spencer he grinned at me and did a double thumbs-up. 'Mum and Dad have already bought the house,' he said.

I ran over and gave Mum a huge hug. 'You've bought it?' I yelled. 'You've actually bought it?'

'Well, I'm glad to see *somebody's* pleased,' she said wearily. 'Chelsea wasn't exactly over the moon.'

'It's four against one,' said Spencer philosophically, 'so she'll just have to get over it.'

I wish I had his optimism. Chelsea doesn't have a very good track record in getting over major things. And believe me, she's going to see this as major.

Mum explained that she'd fallen in love with the house the first time she saw it (which was last week), but they'd had to move fast and buy it before they could show it to us because there were loads of developers after it, wanting to turn it into flats, and Mum couldn't bear the thought of that.

Eventually Spencer and I wandered out the front door. I was half expecting to see Chelsea sulking in the back of the car and I was going to persuade her to come and explore the garden with us. But there was no sign of her and I supposed she'd either gone shopping or caught the bus home. Mum would be cross because she doesn't like us going off without telling her where we're going.

Spencer and I made our way round the back and had a good look at the garden. Beyond the yard outside the kitchen was a bit of garden which had obviously been some sort of kitchen garden, although it's hopelessly overgrown now. There were paths leading between raised beds with a high wall on one side, then there were some greenhouses and some steps down to a lawn. On the right was a big hedge with a gap halfway down it and, when we went through, we found ourselves in an orchard with a summer house tucked away in the corner.

'Not too shabby,' said Spencer, although actually it was and the grass hadn't seen a mower all summer. There were some nice apples on the trees though and we were both munching on one as we made our way back to the house. I kept a good look out but I didn't see the cat again. It must have gone home.

There was a house on either side of ours, but with the

high walls and trees they weren't very visible. I wondered who lived in them and what sort of neighbours they'd make and if there were any children in them. I wasn't sure I wanted to leave the estate where we knew everyone and move here where we didn't even know who the neighbours were. They didn't look like the kind of houses you could just pop into for a cup of tea and a chat. They looked like the kind of houses where you'd need a gilt-framed invitation to get in the front door.

But then I looked up and saw the bay window that belonged to my new bedroom. I thought about our house on the estate where we were always on top of each other and I thought about Chelsea's snoring and her inability to put anything away, and I thought: It doesn't really matter about the neighbours because I'm finally going to get a room to myself.

When we got home, Chelsea was in her pyjamas, curled up on the sofa watching telly. As soon as we walked in she got up and swept past us without saying a word. We heard the bedroom door slam and then the unmistakable beat of some of her more aggressive music.

We were all standing in the hallway looking up the stairs. Mum and Dad looked worried. I was cross. We should have been celebrating and instead we were all concerned about Chelsea. I was fed up with Chelsea and her tantrums. Why does she have to be such a drama queen? She's such a brat. I wish she'd go away. We'd make a much better family without her.

I took the details about the new house out of Mum's handbag and went round to see Lauren.

Pam smiled when she answered the door and before she sent me up to Lauren's room I told her about Hill House.

'Oh, that's lovely,' she said, looking at the details. 'Your mum must be over the moon. You know, we used to walk past those houses when we were your age and I always had to drag your mum away because she'd stop at the gates and gaze at them. I bet she can't believe she's going to be living in one!'

I like to think about Mum and Pam being friends like me and Lauren are. For one bizarre moment I wondered if, one day, my daughter would be going round to Lauren's house to play with her daughter. But it was such a strange thought, that one day I'd be grown up and as old as Pam and Mum, that I couldn't quite get my head round it.

Lauren wasn't quite as pleased as her mum had been about the house because she didn't want me to move away. But she did listen as I told her about my new room and I said she could help me decorate it. Mum and Dad had said we could all have a certain amount of money to spend on our new rooms and we could choose what we wanted in them.

Pam invited me to stay for tea and we all watched *The X Factor* and had a good laugh, but I felt kind of hollow. I couldn't stop thinking about how it might be the last time I 'just popped round to Lauren's'.

Friday 8th October

Mum left some boxes in my and Chelsea's bedroom and I've filled six of them with all my stuff. I've decided to have a clear out at the other end because there are a lot of things I ought to get rid of. I couldn't believe how many fluffy toys I have, not to mention the odd Barbie doll I'd found under the bed. One box contained my books and I was itching to get them on the bookshelves in my new room. I stacked the boxes neatly against one wall, which made opening the door a bit tricky. The problem wasn't helped by the fact that Chelsea was being messier than ever and the floor was ankle deep in clothes.

When I realised she wasn't going to make any attempt to pack her own stuff, I spent a couple of hours throwing her things into boxes, only to come to bed to find that she'd tipped the whole lot out again. Well, that's the last time I'm going to help her with anything. Mum will have to sort it out.

Monday 18th October

The 'last time' feeling stayed with me all last week. Walking to school with Lauren, nipping into the newsagent's together for sweets on the way home – everything has taken on a new, nostalgic feeling. Neither of us has said anything about it to each other, but I know Lauren feels the same way because we've both been acting extra silly. When we're at school it's okay because everything's the same there. It's just on the way to and from school when it becomes difficult and I get a lump in my throat.

The house is full of cardboard boxes and the removal van has been booked. Mum said we barely needed one as she's going to have to buy new furniture for Hill House.

The removal men, Terry and his son Baz, came round the other evening to assess the job and Chelsea had been very taken with Baz. She'd even offered to make them a cup of tea, and she and Baz spent half an hour chatting in the garden while Terry discussed the move with Mum and Dad.

He's about eighteen and quite good-looking if you ignore all his tattoos, which was a bit difficult as he was wearing a sleeveless T-shirt so he could show them off. I thought they were repulsive because they made his arms all blue – unless that was just the effect of wearing nothing but a vest in October. Despite all this, Chelsea had homed in on Baz's bare muscular arms like a moth to a bare light bulb.

It looks like we'll be practically camping in the new house for a while until it all gets sorted out. I think it sounds like fun but Chelsea had another major strop when she found out we were going to move before the new house was fully modernised. I've got a feeling Mum and Dad aren't planning to modernise it quite as much as she's hoping, which is fine by me because I think it's perfect as it is.

Saturday 23rd October

In the end, Mum had to do all Chelsea's packing. It became obvious, this morning, that Chelsea didn't intend to do anything. And I mean *anything*. She wouldn't even get out of bed. I didn't like to snitch on her but by nine o'clock, when she still wasn't up, and the removal van was coming at ten, I thought I'd better bring it to Mum's notice.

Mum, who was stressed anyway, stormed into our bedroom and started to fling things any old how into the boxes. Chelsea was just a lump underneath the duvet. I watched from the door as Mum kept up a running commentary.

'How can one girl possibly need so many pairs of shoes? Charlotte, pass me that box. I'm going to fill it with stuff for the charity shop.' I could see the twinkle in her eye as she went through Chelsea's wardrobe. 'I'm sure this top can't fit you any more, Chelsea. Perhaps you'd like it, Charlotte? What do you think?'

There was the faintest of movements from beneath the duvet. Chelsea hates me anywhere near her clothes. She must have been dying to take a look to see which of her precious tops Mum was about to give away.

'What's this?' said Mum, picking Chelsea's favourite top off the floor. It was the one Chelsea had bought on the day after Mum's lottery win, when she'd been in such a good mood. 'This one looks like an old rag, I don't think even the charity shop will want this,' said Mum, knowing full well that the tears were an intentional fashion statement. Chelsea must have known which top Mum was talking about.

'Charlotte, nip downstairs and get me a bin liner. Some of these things need to go straight in the bin.'

Well, that did have an effect but probably not in the way Mum had hoped. Chelsea didn't emerge from under the duvet, at least not much of her, just an arm. It shot out and grabbed the top from Mum's hand and the arm and Chelsea's prized top disappeared under the duvet.

I ran downstairs to get the bin liner because there was a lot of rubbish under all those clothes. Old tissues covered in make-up and glossy magazines still lay in drifts against the skirting boards. Luckily the bin liners were on top of the kitchen worktop. Everything else had disappeared into boxes. The house seemed oddly bare with nothing but boxes stacked everywhere. Mum and Pam were going to come in tomorrow and give the place a good clean.

When I got back upstairs, Mum had made some headway. My bed had been stripped and the wardrobe and chest of drawers were now empty. Mum looked at the mess on top of the dressing table then unceremoniously swiped the whole lot into a box. The sound of Chelsea's make-up, lotions, perfumes and hair gunk products all hitting the bottom of the box didn't even get a twitch from the bed. I started to fill the bin liner with rubbish. I found the white and gold bikini under the chest of drawers and slipped it into the bin liner. If Chelsea never saw it again she wouldn't have to be reminded of Sophie's awful party.

Dad appeared in the doorway holding a screwdriver. 'Right, let's get these beds dismantled,' he said cheerily.

Mum silently indicated the problem to him.

He nodded and taking a corner of the duvet, he pulled. He might as well have tried to remove a limpet from a rock at low tide. Chelsea was not about to give it up.

'Seems like this bed is going to have to go in the van as it is,' said Dad in a loud voice. 'I don't suppose Terry and Baz will be too happy about it.'

There was a stirring from beneath the duvet. Dad had hit the jackpot all right. The thought of Baz carrying her and the bed down to the removal van was too awful for Chelsea to contemplate. Mum hustled us tactfully out of the room so that Chelsea could emerge, without losing dignity, and get dressed.

The move was so chaotic none of us had time to get

too sentimental about leaving the old house and I was the only one who glanced back when the car turned the corner at the end of our street.

Wednesday 27th October

It's funny sleeping in my old bed without the other one on top. Dad dismantled them in the end and they're now two separate beds instead of bunk beds. They've come with us to the new house because we haven't bought new ones yet and, for the first few nights, I had a problem getting to sleep because of the yawning space above my head.

I've discovered that if I sleep with my head under the duvet it helps. I keep my bedside lamp on all night because being on my own is so weird. I am also very conscious that I'm a long way from any of the others, stuck at the back of the house, as my room is. I make sure that the door to Morticia's boudoir is always firmly shut, because I don't much like walking past it in the dark if I have to get up to go to the loo in the middle of the night.

After the third night of waking up with a beating heart

because I thought I heard scratching at the window, I'm beginning to wonder if that fortune card was right and you should be careful what you wish for. I'd give anything to go and get into Mum and Dad's bed but I'm way too old for that. Besides, I've been harping on about having my own room for so long it would be way too embarrassing to admit that, now I've got it, I've discovered I'm terrified of the dark.

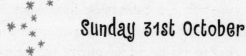

Sunday 31st October

The half-term week has gone far too quickly. Lauren and Pam came over yesterday to see the new house. I had hoped that Lauren could stay over for the night but Mum said to wait until the house is sorted out. Apparently there's a new family in our old house already.

Lauren didn't seem too impressed by my new bedroom. I know it looks a bit old-fashioned at the moment, but I didn't tell her I like it as it is in case she thinks I'm being weird. She didn't want to go and explore the garden or help me pick out a new bed for my room. I think she's still sulking because I've moved away – as if it was my fault! Which got me thinking about those wishes again and how it might actually be my fault, but there was no way I could explain to Lauren about Gypsy Ginny.

I wish I could have another week off school so I can get

used to living in our new house. I love it. I love sitting by the Aga in the kitchen while Mum cooks and best of all I love the fact that, if there's something on telly I don't want to watch, I can just go in the other room and read my book and I can't even hear the telly. Chelsea's been on at Mum and Dad to give us our own tellies in our bedrooms, but Mum says if they did that they'd never see any of us again. In Chelsea's case that would surely be a good thing. Maybe, when we get our new HD flatscreen, I can persuade Mum and Dad to let Chelsea have the old one.

Monday 1st November

Back to school today.

I was on my own this morning because Spencer catches an earlier bus and Chelsea was going in later.

I was a bit nervous. Lauren and I used to catch a bus into town sometimes, but I've never had to get one on my own before. As it turned out, I wasn't completely alone because when I got to the bus stop there were loads of Avon Comp kids there. I did a quick recce to see if there was anyone I knew. There was a girl who I was sure was in my form, but I couldn't for the life of me remember her name. She was fairly overweight and had stringy ginger hair and – embarrassingly – knee-length socks and sensible shoes. She saw me looking and smiled shyly at me. I decided it would be social suicide to get too pally with her so I kept my distance. Also, I didn't want to turn up at school with a 'new best friend' and upset Lauren, who might think I was abandoning her and who would have had to walk to school on her own now, if she missed Karly and Tiffany.

I needn't have bothered being so sensitive about Lauren's feelings, as it turned out. When I got to school I was earlier than I would have been walking from the estate so I hung around the gate, waiting impatiently for Lauren to arrive. She finally turned up, walking slowly and chatting avidly to a girl I'd never seen before. When Lauren eventually saw me she waved and came hurrying over.

'Hey, Charlotte, this is Stacy. Guess where she lives.' I must have looked blank. 'In your old house!' said Lauren triumphantly, like she was pulling a rabbit out of a hat. Actually Stacy does look a bit like a rabbit. She has abnormally large teeth, and her eyes are impossibly huge. Maybe she is half Manga.

What's wrong with me? Why am I suddenly being so judgemental about everyone today?

'Isn't that amazing?' continued Lauren. 'She moved in last week.'

I took a couple of steps backwards so I could get a good look at Stacy. She's way taller that me (but then isn't everyone?) and nearly a head taller than Lauren, and far too skinny – all angles. She had the faintest touch of make-up on, just a bit of mascara and lip gloss. Not enough to get told off for. I reckoned she'd be in Year 9 or 10 so with any luck she'd disappear when the bell went. I don't know why but she made me feel uncomfortable. Maybe it was the cool, assessing look she gave me.

When the bell finally rang and we trooped inside for registration, I kept expecting Stacy to peel off and go her own way. When she followed us into our form room I realised, with a sinking, sick feeling, that she wasn't going anywhere. As if that wasn't bad enough, she plonked herself down in *my* seat, the one right next to Lauren. I waited about four heartbeats for Lauren to say something but she didn't. I didn't want to cause a scene by saying 'Oi, that's my seat,' so I sat round the corner of the square table on the other side of Lauren. Lauren did all the talking. Stacy didn't say anything and I had a strange lump somewhere between my heart and my mouth which was stopping me from speaking, so Lauren chatted away oblivious to her two silent friends.

I learnt, before Mr Lawson came in, that Stacy had moved from London with her mum and older brother and younger sister. I wondered idly how they'd managed to jump the queue on the council housing list. I knew from what Mum had said that the Bristol waiting list for a council house was about as long as the Gloucester Road. It didn't seem fair that someone from London should waltz in and grab one. I had to tell myself off again for being so judgemental.

I did remember to keep a look out for the girl I'd seen at the bus stop. She *was* sitting in our form room and I'm slightly ashamed of myself for not really having noticed her before. When Mr Lawson read out the register I waited for her name to come up, even though Lauren was trying to whisper something to me at the time. I had to ignore her in order to catch the girl quietly saying yes to the name Annabel. Lauren immediately turned to Stacy to whisper to her instead so I wished I hadn't ignored her; it wasn't that important. When I turned back, Stacy and Lauren were giggling together. I felt unfairly cross with Annabel for having distracted me.

Things got worse after registration because the first lesson was maths. I silently prayed that Stacy wasn't some kind of maths whizz and would go off with Lauren to the top set. 'Please let her be a bit rubbish and not in the top set,' I chanted to myself.

Lauren picked up her bag. 'I'm off now. Make sure you look after Stacy for me, Charlotte. She's in your group for maths. See you in English.' And she was gone.

Stacy smiled at me. 'Sorry to be such a pain,' she said. 'I hate being new and totally clueless.'

Her sudden change to sweet and friendly took me totally off guard. Any thoughts of going off without her and leaving her stranded were dashed. After all, it wasn't her fault she was new, and it must be really difficult coming into a school where everyone knows everyone else. But there are plenty of other people she could attach herself to. I made up my mind to introduce her to a few of them.

Stacy chatted away about the house all the way to maths. 'It's so nice not to be living in a flat any more,' she said. 'And the Ratcliffe estate is way nicer than the estate we lived on in London. I hardly dared leave the flat sometimes, it was so bad. Someone got stabbed once practically outside our front door.'

I made an appropriately sympathetic noise, even though I wasn't sure whether or not to believe her.

By the time maths was over, I'd decided that Stacy wasn't too bad after all. It was fun to have someone to giggle with in the back row. Stacy drew a really funny cartoon of Miss Carlisle. It had me in fits and for a moment we thought Miss Carlisle was going to demand to see what it was that was distracting us. Luckily she was too busy telling off some of the boys so we got away with it. But I did make sure I got into the classroom before Stacy for the next lesson so that I could get my usual seat next to Lauren.

When it was time to go home, I nearly turned left at the school gates with Lauren and Stacy before I remembered that I had to go the other way to get the bus.

'See you tomorrow,' called Stacy cheerfully, linking arms with Lauren. Stacy sounded friendly enough but what Lauren didn't see was the sly smile she was giving me. I must have looked as dejected as I felt because Lauren smiled at me and unlinked her arm from Stacy's. I didn't look back as I set off for the bus stop but I didn't really need to. The image of Stacy walking along next to Lauren was burned into my brain, and I'd got a pretty bad headache coming on.

I managed to get off the bus at the right stop. Annabel got off there as well. I ducked into the mini supermarket next to the bus stop, thinking that I could buy some sweets, and by the time I came out she'd have gone and it would avoid any awkwardness of walking with her. My way was blocked by a fat shop assistant. 'You can't come in here with that,' he said, pointing to my rucksack.

'What?'

He pointed to a sign on the wall. *No more than two school children at a time and NO school bags.* Is that even legal? What are we supposed to do with our bags? Leave them on the pavement outside? I walked out, deeply offended. Obviously the shop must have had some problems with school kids pinching stuff, but that didn't mean we were all like that. I objected to being treated like some sort of criminal.

I stomped off up the hill.

This hill is going to be a pain. Literally. The backs of my legs were burning before I was even halfway up. I could see Annabel ahead of me and the gap between us was shortening. I slowed down. But it was no good; I'd have had to stop in order not to catch up with her. I wondered if she knew I was behind her and was going slow in the hope that I would catch her up. When I finally reached her I saw that this probably wasn't the case. She was bright red in the face and breathing heavily.

'Hi there, Annabel,' I said, giving in to the inevitable. It would have been rude just to walk past her.

Annabel pushed her glasses back up her nose and peered at me. 'Hi.' I think she would have blushed if she hadn't been so red anyway; she was obviously painfully shy. I could see conversation was going to be difficult. We carried on walking at her snail's pace.

She smiled at me. 'It's nice to have someone to walk with. It helps to take my mind off the agony.'

Oh God, I hoped she didn't think I was about to become her new best buddy. As if she could read my mind she added, 'It's okay. I won't talk to you at school or anything.'

That made me feel really bad. Was I that obvious? And why shouldn't she talk to me at school? But I knew what the others would say if she did. I could hear their cutting remarks about her appearance in my head. It only made my headache worse and I was glad when we reached the top of the hill where I turned left and Annabel turned right.

Tomorrow I'd find out where she lived. I'd ask her about her family. She was right; it did make the walk less tedious having someone to talk to. I might even say hi to her at school. Maybe. If there's no one else around.

I was thinking all this as I walked along our street and was so absorbed that I nearly missed the little white cat. She was sitting outside the gate of the house next door to ours. I slowed down so as not to frighten her and I thought she was going to let me stroke her, but just as I got close enough she bolted away. I stopped at the open gate and looked up the driveway. It wasn't as long as ours and it didn't have a bend in it, so I had a good view of the house. It was a big house with two large bay windows either side of the front door. There were five steps leading up to the door. The garden was untidy and overgrown but where our house had a front lawn, this house was all tarmac at the front. I noticed that beside the front door were about five doorbells, all with a name below them.

As I stood there staring, the door opened and a man came out. He was wearing grease-covered jeans and holding a spanner in one hand. It was then that I noticed a big motorbike parked on the tarmac. Sitting beside the motorbike and washing her paws was the cat.

The man saw me staring and raised his hand in a greeting. I raised mine back. I know you shouldn't talk to strange men but he was our neighbour after all.

'Is that your cat?' I called up the drive. He bent down to stroke it and the cat twined itself round his ankles. I was wondering whether or not to go up the drive so that he didn't have to shout his answer, when the front door opened again and a woman came out. She was carrying two mugs and she came down the steps gracefully, despite the big boots she was wearing, and handed one of the mugs to the man.

She saw me and waved and called out, 'Hi.'

Feeling bold, I went halfway up the drive. The woman looked nice and she was still smiling at me so I carried on. On closer inspection the couple weren't as young as I'd thought. The woman had blond hair that was definitely bleached and she'd grown it into long dreadlocks. It was bunched together at the back with a massive scrunchy. Apart from the big boots, she was wearing a short skirt and a vest top under a floaty top with a big cardigan, which looked like something Grumps would wear. Somehow, she managed to look amazing in it.

'You must be Charlotte,' she said. 'I was talking to your

mum this morning. I'm glad she bought the house. There were a load of developers after it who wanted to turn it into flats, like this one.' She indicated the house behind her.

They were really friendly and we chatted for a while. She's called Belinda and the man, who hardly said anything, is called Chris. It's a relief to know that the new neighbours are so nice. It made me realise just how much I'd been worrying that they'd be snooty and stand-offish and that we'd never fit in here.

But I still had a bad headache so I was hopping from foot to foot with impatience to get home, so they probably think *I'm* deranged.

When I got home I remembered that I'd forgotten to ask them about the cat. So when I walked into the kitchen and saw the cat sitting by the Aga, washing its paws, I thought for a minute that I was seeing things.

Mum was in there, and from the smell I guessed she'd been making cookies. Mum's cookies are the best ever. She puts chocolate chips and fudge chips in them and they're always soft in the middle. The one she handed me was still warm and I took a big bite which meant that I then couldn't ask her about the cat, so I just pointed at it and raised my eyebrows.

'Oh yes,' said Mum, 'apparently that cat lives here. I was talking to the neighbours earlier. They tried to look after it when the old man went into a home but it kept coming back here. They've been feeding it but it won't move in with them, so it looks like we're stuck with it.'

My first instinct was to rush over and give the cat a huge hug, but I got the feeling it would have been insulted. You have to be careful and respectful of cats and earn their trust gradually. I wanted to tell Mum how pleased I was that we now had a pet cat but I was having trouble swallowing my mouthful of cookie.

Mum glanced at the half finished biscuit and then at me. 'Are you feeling okay?' she asked.

In truth, I wasn't. I wanted to stay and talk to Mum about the new neighbours and Annabel and Stacy but I didn't have the energy.

'Actually, I feel a bit rough,' I told her. 'My throat hurts and I've got a really bad headache.'

Mum came and felt my forehead. 'Oh dear, I think you're coming down with something.'

Thursday 4th November

Mum was right. I've been really ill. I had to have the rest of the week off school. The first two days I spent in bed with a temperature and fever. I couldn't help thinking it served me right for wishing I could have some more time at home. I know I'm being stupid but I can't help noticing that every time I accidentally make a wish, it somehow comes true. I've drawn a new height line on my bedroom door frame and every night I say, 'I wish I was taller,' before I get into bed.

Spencer poked his head round the door to see if I was all right earlier but he wouldn't come in and chat. He said he didn't want to catch my lurgy because he didn't want to miss any school. He must really like that new school of his. If he was still at Avon Comp he'd be in here like a shot trying to pick up my bugs so he could get time off.

It hasn't exactly been peaceful in the house this week

because Mum and Dad have got the builders in. They're turning the downstairs loo and boot room into a shower room. Because my bedroom is at the back of the house it's fairly quiet in here and Missy, which is what I've called our new cat, has been hiding in my room because of the disruption downstairs.

Yesterday my temperature had gone down and I ventured downstairs with my duvet and snuggled up on the sofa in front of the telly. I fell asleep watching an old black and white film and woke up at half past two when the builders started drilling just down the corridor. I waited until after three o'clock when I reckoned Lauren would be home, then phoned her. I wanted all the gossip from school and to find out what I'd missed. I was surprised she hadn't rung me at all. When we were in the old house she used to come round every night to check I was okay whenever I was ill. Annoyingly her mobile was switched off so I rang her house. Her mum answered and said Lauren wasn't there and would be back around six. I was dying to ask Pam where she'd gone but it sounded unnaturally nosy, so I just said I'd ring back later.

As I put the phone down Spencer arrived home. I was hoping he'd come and watch telly with me and tell me about his new school but he said he had homework and disappeared upstairs. I've hardly seen Spencer since we moved. He only seems to come out of his room to eat and go to school.

Then I had the idea that perhaps Lauren wasn't home because she was coming to visit me. But wouldn't her mum have said something? Unless it was a surprise. Maybe she'd turn up any minute. It only took twenty minutes on the bus.

By four o'clock I decided she probably wasn't coming. By five o'clock I was certain she wasn't coming but I still positioned myself on the sofa so that I could see down the drive. By six o'clock I knew she definitely wasn't coming. I waited until ten past before I rang her again. This time she picked up the phone.

'Hi,' I said.

'Oh, it's you.'

I waited but she didn't ask me how I was or if I was better so I came straight to the point.

'I rang earlier but you were out. Where did you go?'

'Oh, you know . . .'

'No.' I didn't know, obviously, or I wouldn't have asked. If she'd gone round to Stacy's, like I was beginning to suspect, why didn't she just tell me?

'Nowhere special. Anyway, how are you?' she finally enquired, though I got the feeling it was more to change the subject than because she actually cared. We talked about school for a bit then she said she had to go because it was her teatime.

'Why don't you come round Friday night?' I said. 'We could get a film and I'll ask Mum if you can stay the night.'

I didn't really think Mum would agree as I was ill but I hoped I could persuade her on the grounds that it would make me feel better.

'I can't come on Friday,' said Lauren. 'I've got something

on after school, but I'll come and see you on Saturday and bring you all the work you've missed.'

'Thanks,' I said, but I think my sarcastic tone was lost on her.

After we'd said goodbye, I hung up and stood there wondering what Lauren's got on tomorrow night that's more important than visiting her best friend.

Chelsea arrived home then, and I realised how I hadn't seen much of her either. She'd stopped sulking in her room and now she seemed to be out all the time. I wondered where she went, but there was no point asking her because I was sure she wouldn't tell me.

She looked different, I thought; sort of rich. She'd had her hair cut and I noticed her nails were done. And was that a tan . . . ? Mum will go spare if she thinks Chelsea has been to a tanning salon. It's more likely to be out of a bottle. I'm pretty sure she's hanging out on the estate with the girls from the flats, and by the look of it, they were spending all their time preening.

'What are you staring at?' Chelsea said to me.

'You look like you've just spent a week in Spain,' I told her.

'Huh, chance would be a fine thing,' she said and disappeared up to her room.

Friday 5th November

It just occurred to me, when I wrote today's date: Bonfire Night! That's why Lauren can't come tonight – because she's probably going to the bonfire and fireworks that they always have down at the community centre on the Ratcliffe estate. Why didn't she just say so? Am I being overly paranoid or was she keeping quiet because she doesn't want me turning up? I know it's for Ratcliffe estate residents only but surely I could go. I mean Grumps still lives there and he could take me. When I suggested this to Mum, though, she said there was no way I was going out because, if I was too ill to go to school, I was too ill to go to a bonfire party.

Spencer and I watched the fireworks going off randomly all over the city from his bedroom window. I tried not to think about Lauren having a good time with Stacy back home on the estate. Funny how I still think of the estate as home. Maybe Sophie was right and you can never take the estate out of the girl.

When I got into bed I checked my phone and there was a message from Lauren. It said: *Meet me tomoz 12.30 outside Harvey Nicks.*

We don't usually go there – it's in the oh so posh Cabot Circus and we usually go to The Galleries. Not that it matters. I'm just happy I'm finally going to get to spend the day with Lauren without Stacey getting in the way. It'll be just like old times.

Saturday 6th November

I think I have just experienced the worst day in the whole of my life. I wasn't going to write about it because it was so awful and I don't ever want to be reminded of it; but I need to put it down so I can make some sort of sense of it. What just happened? I've got a feeling I've been totally stitched up.

First, it took me all morning to persuade Mum that I was well enough to go out. I had to do loads of chores to convince her.

I got to town a bit early so I walked around the shops for a while and then went and stood in front of Harvey Nichols. I was so busy looking for Lauren that I didn't notice Stacy until she was right in front of me. At first I didn't recognise her because she had so much make-up on. Her mascara was so thick it made me shudder just to look at her eyelashes. Like her eyes aren't big enough in the first place. Now she looked more like an owl than a rabbit – her fake nails looked like talons. In fact, *I* began to feel like the rabbit; frozen in horror. Why does she always have this effect on me?

Then a horrid thought occurred to me. Had Lauren invited her along as well? God! Why would she do that? Was I the only one who found Stacy creepy and repellent? Well, when Lauren turned up I'd make my excuses and go home. Then again, that would make me look like a wet blanket and it would mean that they would be together having a fun time. I wasn't going to go down without a fight if Stacy thought she could waltz in and take my best friend.

'Lauren's not here,' she said.

It took a few moments for this to sink in. 'Oh.' I couldn't think what else to say.

Stacy gave me that sweet smile of hers and linked arms with me. 'She'll be along later but she wants me to look after you until she gets here.' She soon dropped my arm though. The height difference made it too uncomfortable for her. We must have looked like an odd pair; me so short and her so tall.

For the next couple of hours we looked round the shops. Or rather Stacy did and I tagged along wondering when Lauren was going to turn up. I tried to call her when Stacy went to the loo, but she must have had her phone switched off because it went straight to voicemail. I didn't bother leaving her a message. I'd try again later.

Stacy was totally into clothes. We must have gone into every clothes shop we passed and tried on every single thing in every shop. At least that's what it felt like. I did make her go into Waterstone's but she got bored after about ten seconds and said, 'What's the point of books? It's bad enough that we have to read them at school. God, don't they sell magazines in here? It's okay for you. You can afford to waste your money.' So I gave up.

Stacy hadn't actually bought anything all day and she'd been making comments about how nice it must be to be rich and be able to afford anything you wanted. I ignored all these remarks because I know they were aimed at me. Actually, I did have quite a bit in my bank account which Dad had helped me open because I'm saving up my pocket money so I can get Spencer a birthday present and that War Hammer stuff is really expensive.

I decided that I was going to head off home. If Lauren wanted to shop with Stacy then she was welcome to her. I'd had enough. If she made one more remark about what *she'd* do if *her* mum had won the lottery and what *she'd* buy I might just end up hitting her.

'I've got go now,' I told Stacy.

Then, just at that moment Stacy said, 'Oooh, that's my phone vibrating,' and got it out of her pocket. 'It's Lauren. She says she's on her way and we're to meet her in Starbucks in half an hour.' I was tempted to go home anyway but decided I could probably survive another half hour. Perhaps I could persuade Lauren to get rid of Stacy so we could have our usual shopping trip which didn't involve every clothes shop in Bristol. We liked to mooch around in The Body

Shop and Lush, trying out all the free samples and usually ended up smelling like a fruit salad. It was fun just buying little things like pens and hair slides and chocolate. Trailing round looking at clothes was not my idea of a good time. I could do that with my mum.

And that's when it got weird.

Stacy had dragged me into a changing room with her. She was going on and on about how great the clothes were and how she *had* to have them. I wasn't paying too much attention except to notice that she might be tall but she didn't have much of a chest to speak of. And then Stacy grabbed *my* bag and started stuffing the clothes into it.

'What are you doing?' I squeaked.

'Don't panic,' she said, 'it's dead simple. Look.' She opened her bag and pulled out a library book. 'When we walk out the shop and the alarm goes off, I stop and wait for the assistant then tell her that my library book has set the alarm off. See?'

I was busy pulling the clothes out of my bag. 'There is no way you're putting those in my bag,' I told her.

'Don't be so chicken,' she hissed. 'I used to do it all the time in London. It's easy.'

'It's stealing!'

'It's all right for you to preach! You can afford to buy them. Well, we're not all as lucky as you. I'm not leaving this shop without them so, if you won't have them in your bag, you'll have to do the explaining about the library book,' she said, thrusting it at me.

I still don't know why I didn't just tell her that I didn't have to do anything if I didn't want to and then walk out. It might have had something to do with the fact that she was standing between me and the cubicle door, but I wonder if it was also because I did actually feel slightly guilty.

In fact, it was at that moment I realised I've been feeling guilty ever since we won the lottery. I don't know why. I just have. Like we didn't deserve it or something, or maybe going from poor to rich over night takes a bit of adjusting to (not that Chelsea seems to have a problem adjusting, or Spencer for that matter. What's wrong with me?) Anyhow, the upshot was I ended up buying the clothes. Stupid, I know, but at the time it seemed like the sanest thing to do. Stacy just stood there grinning while I paid for them with my new debit card.

'Oh, Charlotte, that's so kind of you. Thank you. You didn't have to, you know.'

Yeah, right.

When we finally got out of the shop I stormed off in the direction of Starbucks and Stacy, following behind said, 'Oh, there goes my phone again.'

Just wait until Lauren hears about this, I was thinking. This will put her off Stacy for sure.

'Lauren can't come after all,' said Stacy. 'What a shame. Still, we've had fun, haven't we? Do you fancy a coffee in Starbucks anyway?'

I can't remember exactly what I said but it had to do with me going home immediately. Stacy didn't argue. I guess she'd got what she wanted.

The minute I got home I tried ringing Lauren's house but there was no reply. I was standing in the hall, biting my nails and wondering how I could get hold of Lauren when Mum came out of the passage door.

'Charlotte! Where did you go? I thought you'd gone to meet Lauren.'

'I did.'

'So how come she turned up here with the work you missed last week? What is going on?'

I mumbled something about there being a mix up and shot up to my room.

Now I've written it all down some things are a bit clearer. Firstly, Lauren obviously doesn't know anything about my trip into town today or why would she have turned up here? In that case, it can't have been her who texted me last night telling me to meet her. Obviously it was Stacy. What's more, Stacy must have Lauren's phone.

Now I think about it, I've never seen Stacy with a mobile phone at school and the one she kept getting out today was identical to Lauren's. So all those texts she kept getting from Lauren were made up to keep me from going home. The phone was switched off, which is why it didn't ring when I tried to call Lauren. And why didn't I wonder why Lauren kept calling Stacy instead of me?

I feel so stupid, the whole day was one big set-up. And I fell for it. I can't believe I was stupid enough to buy those clothes for Stacy. What was I thinking? That must have been her intention all along: to get 'the rich kid' to fork out.

But something else is bothering me. That story about the library book setting the alarms off. If that was true, why didn't the alarms go off every time we went in and out of the shops? And if it wasn't true, that must mean that Stacy was setting me up to get caught for shoplifting. If everything had gone according to her plan, it would have been me with the clothes in my bag and I don't doubt for a minute that she would have acted all innocent. Why would she do that to me?

Lauren obviously doesn't know anything about all this so I need to get hold of her and tell her about the shoplifting and how Stacy nicked her phone. Then maybe she'll realise what a freak Stacy is and stop being friends with her.

Sunday 7th November

I've been trying to get hold of Lauren all day. It's been driving me completely mad. Her mobile is still switched off and there was no answer on her landline all morning. Then her mum picked up the phone in the afternoon and said Lauren was out. I'm sure Pam didn't sound as friendly as she usually is. Maybe it's because she found out that I wasn't here yesterday when Lauren came to drop my homework off. Or maybe it's just my paranoid imagination working overtime. If I didn't get to talk to Lauren soon I was going to go mental. Was she avoiding me?

I tried again at eight this evening, thinking she must be back by then, what with school tomorrow; but her dad said she wasn't. I'll just have to sort it out with her tomorrow.

Monday 8th November

I wasn't feeling too good this morning, but I pretended I was completely better because I wanted to go to school and tell Lauren what had happened.

I said hello to Annabel at the bus stop and she asked me how I was, which was nice of her, but I didn't sit with her on the bus. When we got off, I walked to school with her because I thought it would be rude not to. I was hoping Lauren wouldn't see us arriving together but Annabelle said goodbye when we got to the gates, which was a relief. I was worried she was going to hang around and Lauren would tease me about my 'new friend'. As it turned out I needn't have worried.

Eventually Karly and Tiffany arrived but they said they hadn't seen Lauren and Stacy. I didn't like the way they said 'Lauren and Stacy' like they were saying Laurel and Hardy or Ant and Dec. I told myself to stop being paranoid, but when the bell went and there was still no sign of them I began to wonder if they'd slipped in without my noticing and I'd find them whispering and giggling in the form room. But they weren't in there either. It wasn't until Mr Lawson was taking the register that they turned up, breathless and giggling.

'You're late,' said Mr Lawson. 'Lunchtime detention – room twenty-six, the pair of you.'

Lauren looked mortified. She's never had detention for being late before. I mean, she only lives round the corner and we were never late when *we* came together. Avon Comp has a zero tolerance policy on being late which means an instant detention.

'What happened?' I whispered across to her.

'I couldn't find my shoes, could I, Lauren?' Stacy butted in.

I wanted to tell her to shut up and go away but that would have made *me* look like the horrible one. So instead I tried to steer the conversation around to next weekend because Mum's invited Pam, Gary and Lauren over for Sunday lunch. I was just telling Lauren what I had planned for us to do but Stacy kept pulling funny faces and, when I mentioned how we could explore the garden, Stacy started yawning in a really fake way.

And it was like that for the rest of the day. Every time I asked Lauren something or tried to talk to her, Stacy would butt in. I was desperate to get Lauren on her own so I could tell her about the nightmare shopping trip but it was impossible. Lauren seemed to be avoiding looking at me. In science, when Lauren asked to go to the loo, I was so desperate to talk to her alone I put my hand up and asked to go as well. Of course, the teacher said I'd have to wait until Lauren got back and Stacy gave me a really sly grin. I was so frustrated I could feel tears forming and had to bend over the experiment to hide them, which nearly made me throw up because we were dissecting a heart.

At lunchtime Lauren and Stacy went off to detention together so I had lunch with Karly and Tiffany. That was a complete nightmare as well, because all they wanted to talk about was what it was like to have your mum win the lottery. I wanted to say, 'It's not all it's cracked up to be,' thinking about how it was causing all these problems, but I knew that would sound ungrateful and I couldn't be bothered to explain. I just said it was great which sounded really lame, and they wanted to know if I was going to go on the school skiing trip now. Do I look like someone who can ski? What is wrong with everyone? Why do they think I've morphed into a completely different person all of a sudden?

Because I wanted to change the subject, I asked them what they thought of Stacy.

'She great,' said Karly. 'She said her mum's a hairdresser and she's going to get her to cut my hair next week. She said she's got loads of make-up I can try out as well.'

Probably all nicked from Boots, I couldn't help thinking. I wondered what they'd say if I told them about the shoplifting. I was seriously considering it when Tiffany said, 'Stacy told me she thinks I could be a model. She knows some people in London and she's going to send them some photos of me.'

At this point I gave up. Karly and Tiffany were both under the Stacy spell, but then she wasn't trying to come between them.

By home time I still hadn't managed to speak to Lauren and I was feeling totally fed up. It didn't help that it was raining.

When I got off the bus at the mini-mart and was faced with the hill to climb, I felt really miserable. I was rooting about in the bottom of my bag, looking for my umbrella, when Annabel tapped me on the shoulder.

'Charlotte, could you do me a really big favour?' she asked.

That was the last thing I needed, I thought as I put the umbrella up.

'I really need to go into the shop. Do you think you could hold my bag for me? I won't be long.' She passed me her bag, even though I hadn't said a word, and disappeared into the shop.

I stood on the pavement for what seemed like an hour. I thought she'd only gone in for a Kit Kat or something, but when she finally came out she was lugging two carrier bags stuffed full of food. No wonder she's overweight.

'Sorry,' she said, 'there was a really long queue. That no bag rule is so annoying. If it wasn't for you, I'd have had to go home and then come back again to get the shopping.'

I didn't have the heart to give her bag back so we dragged ourselves up the hill; I was carrying her bag as well as mine and trying to hold the umbrella over both of us.

When we got to the top we stopped outside the Health Spa shop. Annabel put her carrier bags down, put her hood up and I handed her bag back.

'Have you got much further to go?' I asked, wondering if I ought to offer to help her as far as her house.

'No, I'm just round the corner,' she said. 'See you tomorrow.'

I watched her walk away and wondered why she had so much shopping in the first place. I still don't know much about her. I'm sure she's an only child who lives in a big posh house with her mum and dad who are probably quite old and protective or they wouldn't let her out looking like she does with her long white socks, knee-length skirt and sensible shoes. Mind you, at that moment, I was almost envious of her sensible shoes because my little pumps were soaked through. I couldn't wait to get home and dry off.

I thought I might go straight upstairs and get into my pyjamas, but when I let myself in there was a commotion going on in the passage to the kitchen so I went to investigate. Mum, Dad and Spencer were all admiring the new bathroom which the builders had finally finished today. I squeezed through to get a look.

So much for not ruining the authenticity of the house. The new bathroom was seriously modern and it wasn't just a shower room either. There was a corner jacuzzi bath, two sinks as well as a shower and a loo. I noticed there were speakers set into the ceiling. That was it – I had to try the new bath out. I could see Mum was dying to get in there too, but she let me have a go first because I was cold and wet and she was worried I'd get ill again.

I lay in the bath thinking that, if this was what it was like to be a millionaire, then maybe it wasn't all so bad. The bubbles were bubbling around me and it was like they were literally washing all my cares away. I'd ring Lauren later and put her straight about Stacy. In fact, if it wasn't for Stacy, everything would be perfect. I lay back and said loudly, 'I wish Stacy didn't exist.' Then I felt bad. What if Stacy got run over or something because I'd wished she didn't exist? I know I can't stand her but I'd feel terrible if something like that happened and it was all my fault.

A loud knocking on the door brought me to my senses. It was Chelsea demanding that I let her in so she could see the new bathroom. I told her to go away. I might not have big breasts yet or anything else much to speak of, but I wasn't going to have people traipsing through the bathroom while I was in the bath.

I rang Lauren on my mobile when I was all tucked up in my new fluffy dressing gown and sitting on my bed with Missy.

'Hello, Charlotte,' she said, when she finally answered the phone. 'What do you want?'

She definitely sounded frosty but then I had stood her up on Saturday, as far as she knew.

I decided to get straight to the point.

'Listen, you know Stacy?' I began.

'What about Stacy?' said Lauren.

I wasn't going to be put off by her unfriendly tone. 'Well, yesterday we went shopping but —' I was about to explain about the text from Lauren's phone and how I thought I was meeting her in town, not Stacy. But I didn't get any further.

'I know all about your shopping trip. Stacy told me and I know what you're trying to do.'

'What do you mean?' I asked.

'You knew I was coming round and you arranged to meet Stacy and then tried to buy her friendship by buying her all those clothes. You are so pathetic.'

I was speechless but Lauren didn't notice. I could hear giggling in the background. Stacy.

'Did she tell you about the shoplifting?' I shouted down the phone.

'What?' said Lauren.

'Did she tell you that she was going to pinch the clothes from the shop and I had to buy them to stop her

127

getting us into trouble? And did she say how she took your phone and used it to make me think I was meeting *you* in town in the first place?' I knew I wasn't explaining things very well but I was under a lot of pressure here. There was a muffled conversation at the other end but I couldn't make out what they were saying. Then Lauren came back on the line.

'Stacy said you'd try something like this. Of course she didn't have my phone. It was under my bed all the time. She just found it for me. As for that shoplifting thing, you've always had a vivid imagination but I can't believe you expect me to believe that!'

'But it's the truth!' I was shouting with frustration. 'Can't you see what she's doing?'

'You know what? You've changed, Charlotte Johnson, and if that's what having money does to people then I'm glad we haven't got any.' And she hung up on me.

I've been sitting on my bed stroking Missy, who's been purring and rubbing her silky head against my arm. At least there's someone who likes me.

I can't believe Lauren believed all those lies Stacy had told her. And what did she mean *I've changed*? I haven't changed. It's so unfair. She thinks I've changed because of the money but I know I haven't, which means *she's* changed towards me because of the money. I think she's jealous and Stacy knows that so she's encouraging her to think it's all about the money when it isn't.

I hate Stacy, but if she thinks she can get rid of me that easily, she's got another thing coming.

I went to see Spencer because he's always good in a crisis but, when I knocked and opened his bedroom door, it looked like Spencer was having a crisis of his own. He was sitting on his bed surrounded by open books and he looked about as miserable as I felt.

'What's up?' we both said at the same time. Normally that would have had us both in hysterics but today it hardly raised a smile.

'Homework?' I asked, pointing to the books.

'Sort of,' said Spencer.

I looked around his bedroom. It's pretty basic, just a bed, a desk, a wardrobe and a chest of drawers. He had plans to build scenery for his War Hammer collection and have it all out on display. I guess he hasn't had time because of all his homework.

'Alec has signed up for the War Hammer club at school,' I told him. I didn't mention how lonely Alec had looked.

Spencer took his glasses off and rubbed his eyes. He looked worn out.

'Do you still go to the Games Workshop with him on Saturdays?' I asked.

'I haven't been for ages. I haven't had time,' said Spencer.

'I don't think they should give you so much homework

if it means you can't have a life,' I told him. 'Friends are important as well.'

I wished I hadn't said that because it reminded me of Lauren and how she didn't seem to want to be my friend any more.

I will not cry, I told myself, clamping my teeth together and staring at the carpet.

'Hey, what's the matter?' said Spencer, pushing his books and problems aside for me. 'Come on, it can't be that bad.'

So I told him about how Stacy had moved into our old house and was now taking over my best friend and there wasn't anything I could do because we were stuck on this hill away from the estate and everyone liked Stacy anyhow.

I didn't mention the shopping trip because the whole thing would have sounded deranged and I didn't want to admit that I'd been duped so easily.

When I'd finished, I was red in the face and I think Spencer realised that it had been difficult for me to talk about, because it's not easy admitting you're a loser and that your best friend doesn't like you any more.

Spencer could see I was embarrassed but he didn't offer any advice because he's a boy and they don't have best friends, they have mates and hang out in packs.

Instead, he told me how when he got to the new school he found out he wasn't as clever as he'd thought he was and he wasn't the top of the class any more. What he was doing wasn't homework, he was just trying to be better. He looked pretty embarrassed about it and I knew he'd only told me to make me feel better, like we were two losers together.

I couldn't believe it though. Spencer's the cleverest person I know. I was sure he was doing fine and was just a bit put out that he wasn't top in everything.

'Why does it matter if you're not top of the class?' I said. 'It's not like you can't do the work, is it? Can't you just make do with being middle of the class and then you'll have time for other stuff, like your War Hammer and computer games?'

Spencer put his glasses back on and glared at me through them. 'Yeah, and you can always get new friends. You don't have to be friends with Lauren, do you?'

I was about to protest that they were two completely different things when I realised that what Spencer was actually saying was that being top was as important to him as being friends with Lauren was to me.

Then we heard Mum calling us down for tea. I felt much better now I'd told someone and I think Spencer did too because, when we got down to the landing, Chelsea was coming out of her room and Spencer put on his David Attenborough voice and said,

'The dragon occasionally leaves its lair to feed, and to harass and terrify the people.'

Chelsea gave us a withering look and swept past us.

As we went down to the kitchen I decided that maybe

things weren't as bad as I'd thought and that tomorrow everything would be fine. I would be able to tell Lauren what really happened because we've got drama second period and Lauren and I are partners for that. Then Lauren will know what an evil witch Stacy really is.

Tuesday 9th November

Lauren and Stacy pretty much ignored me during registration but I pretended not to notice. I was biding my time until the drama lesson.

The first lesson today was maths and I had to sit next to Stacy because there were no other seats. I could see Annabel sitting at the back next to a geeky boy and decided that I would bribe him to swap seats with me next maths lesson. Maybe I should have confronted Stacy about the lies she told Lauren about me and the shopping trip but somehow I knew it would have been pointless. Besides, I didn't want to talk to her. Ever again. I kept looking at the clock and willing the lesson to end. Then, about halfway through, Stacy handed me a piece of paper. I thought it was going to be a bitchy note or something but, when I looked at it, I saw she'd drawn another of her cartoons and this time it was of Annabel.

I looked at the drawing. It was really cruel. Stacy had made Annabel look way fatter than she actually is and put her in a frilly party frock and, for some reason, had drawn her crying like a baby. Stacy was nudging me and giggling. I pushed the piece of paper back towards her, all the time keeping my eyes on the front of the class. I couldn't even look at Stacy I was so mad. What had Annabel ever done to her?

Stacy was annoyed that I wasn't laughing and admiring her artwork. She scrunched it up into a ball and threw it to Annabel where it landed in front of her on the desk. I twisted round, willing her not to look at it but she must have thought it was a note. My heart leapt to my throat – she might think it was from me! I couldn't look. Stacy was still giggling beside me and I would quite happily have strangled her at that moment.

I sneaked a look at Annabel, expecting to see her crying or at least looking red and upset, but she was totally composed and was staring ahead as if nothing had happened.

I willed the lesson to finish so I could get to drama.

Of course, if I'd known what was going to happen I wouldn't have gone. I'd have pretended I was ill or something, or hidden in the loos. Anything to avoid the humiliation.

When we got to drama, the teacher told us to get into our pairs and work on the scenes that we'd been making up. I went to join Lauren and found Stacy glued to her side. I ignored her, waiting for her to go away but she said, 'You'll

134

have to find another partner. Lauren and I were together last week when you were off sick and we've been working on this at home ever since.'

I looked at Lauren, waiting for her to say something, but she just looked away. Stacy was grinning at me triumphantly and for the second time today I wanted to strangle her. I didn't move for a bit because I didn't know what to do. I always partnered Lauren. Always.

Then the teacher saw me. Stacy had linked arms with Lauren and moved away so I was standing on my own.

'Come on, Charlotte. Find yourself a partner.' I looked around wildly and saw Annabel. I'd have to partner Annabel. But then I saw she already had a partner. I could hear Stacy sniggering behind me.

The teacher came to stand beside me and clapped her hands, then raised her voice above the hubbub.

'Has everyone got a partner?' she shouted. The noise stopped and everyone turned to look at her – and me. 'You'll have to join a pair. Who's going to let Charlotte join them?' she said, looking around.

I could see Stacy out of the corner of my eye, whispering to Lauren but I wasn't going to look at them. I wanted to die, or at the very least cry. My eyes were going all hot. Then I remembered Annabel when she'd seen that drawing and how composed she'd been. I could do that, I thought, holding my head up and staring straight ahead as if I didn't have a care in the world.

There were a few couples who had their hands up. 'Go

and join one of them, then,' said the teacher. She was beginning to sound impatient.

Annabel was looking at me but she didn't have her hand up. She must have thought I had something to do with the horrid cartoon.

Lauren looked as though she was about to raise her hand but Stacy grabbed her arm and held it down. I turned away and went to join Karly and Tiffany.

Somehow I made it through until the end of the day, pretending that nothing cataclysmic had happened.

When the bell finally went and it was home time, I hurried to the bus stop. I wanted to find Annabel and explain to her that I had nothing to do with the cartoon, but she wasn't on the bus and I had to walk up the hill on my own.

Friday 12th November

Dad's lost his job. He's been made redundant. I don't know what he's so upset about. It's not like he needs the money. In fact, that's why he lost his job. His boss said that he had to let someone go and he couldn't do it to any of the others because they had families to support and, while he didn't want to see Dad go, it seemed only fair to get rid of the person who didn't need the job.

Dad's moping about the house and I feel really bad because, if I hadn't made those wishes, we wouldn't have won the lottery and he'd still have a job. Mum's told him he might as well get on with redecorating Morticia's boudoir so that Grandma and Grandpa can come and stay sometime. I nearly told him not to do it because, if they have to sleep in there as it is, you can be sure they'll never come to stay again. But I didn't because I've caused enough trouble as it is.

School was awful today. Lauren and Stacy ignored me again during registration. Karly and Tiffany have cooled towards me as well. I don't know what Lauren's told them but, whatever it is, I know they'll side with her because Ratcliffe girls always stick together and I'm not a Ratcliffe girl any more.

All they could talk about was what they were going to wear next Friday because it's a Wear Your Own Clothes Day in aid of charity. Why are they getting so excited? It's not until next week. Do they need that long to plan it?

I hate it when we have to wear our own clothes to school. It brings me out in a cold sweat. I know that's stupid and it's not like it's important or anything; but this time I just want to blend in, so I can hardly go in Spencer's old cast-offs. There's no way I'm going clothes shopping though. Not even with Mum. The whole thing's making me feel sick. Perhaps I could pretend to be ill and have next Friday off.

At lunchtime I couldn't face going into the canteen on my own. What if I couldn't find anyone to sit with? I didn't want to give Stacy another excuse to laugh at me.

I wandered along the main corridor pretending to be studying the noticeboards. I got to the after-school clubs board and my spirits plummeted even further. It reminded me of when Lauren and I had been friends and couldn't decide on a club. And how we'd decided not to go to one if we couldn't be together. And then I saw it. Her name added to the bottom of the choir list. And above it, naturally, was Stacy's name. I thought I couldn't get any more depressed!

I finally caught up with Annabel on the way home. I had a good complain about Stacy all the way up the hill which made me feel better. I explained that Stacy's cartoon didn't have anything to do with me. When we got to the top I invited her back to my house because I wanted to make sure she knew I wasn't being horrible to her.

'I can't,' she said, 'not tonight.' She looked really disappointed. I was about to say goodbye when she said, 'But you could come to mine, if you want. It's my turn to cook the dinner tonight, though, so you can't stay long.'

'Thanks,' I said.

'That's okay,' said Annabel. I think we both felt a bit awkward.

We turned in at a big gate, a bit like ours, and I saw that, as I'd thought, she lived in an enormous house. But then she led me round the side and up a ramp to a door which had a separate bell. *Flat B – Conners* was written above it. Annabel was looking nervous. 'I don't usually have friends round,' she said. I got the feeling she meant she'd *never* had a friend round. She opened the door with her key and we went inside.

'Mum! I'm home,' called Annabel. 'I've brought a friend.'

Mrs Conners came bustling out into the hall. Or as much as you can bustle when you're in a wheelchair. Annabel introduced me to her mum and then took me to her room. It was very neat and tidy, I noticed, and then realised it would have to be if her mum was going to get in there with her wheelchair. I imagined her coming in to wake Annabel up in the morning, like my mum does. Then I wondered if she did, or if Annabel had to go and help her mum get dressed or something, or was there someone else to do that?

'Is it just you and your mum?' I plucked up the courage to ask.

'Yes,' said Annabel. 'It's always been just me and my mum. That's why I couldn't go back to your place. At least not without a bit of notice. Mum can do most things herself but I have to help out a lot.' I remembered the shopping. And the fact that she had to cook tea tonight.

'There is someone who comes in,' said Annabel, 'but now that I'm older and with the cutbacks and everything, they don't come so often. I could probably come round to yours for a couple of hours tomorrow,' she added hopefully. 'I don't like to go out too much in the evenings during the week because I'm at school all day. Mum's always trying to get me to do more stuff out of the house but I don't like to leave her.'

We spent the rest of the time looking at her books and she lent me a couple of them.

When I left, Annabel came with me because she'd forgotten to pick up some milk on the way home so she'd have to go to the newsagent on the corner of our street to get some. How lucky am I? If I want milk, I just go to the

140

fridge. I never gave a thought as to how it got there. I don't envy Annabel all her extra responsibilities. To think I'd invented a family for Annabel with older parents and a huge house. I really must stop jumping to conclusions about people. You can never tell what someone's like just by looking at them.

We said goodbye outside the shop and, as she went in, Belinda from next door was coming out so I walked the rest of the way home with her.

I didn't say much – I was secretly worrying about Friday and what to wear and hoping that Stacy didn't wear the clothes she'd tricked me into buying for her because that would be too much for me to bear.

'What's up?' said Belinda. 'You look like you want to kill someone.'

Hmm, am I that easy to read? I really must work on my poker face. Anyway, I could hardly tell Belinda about all my problems so in the end I told her about Wear Your Own Clothes Day and how I didn't have anything to wear. I said I hated the way people judged you on what you were wearing.

'It's like that girl I was with just now,' I explained. 'Everyone's really mean to her because she doesn't dress "right".'

'She looks just like I did at her age,' said Belinda. I looked at her, with her long dreadlocks and big boots and little skirt.

'No, really,' said Belinda, laughing. 'I didn't always look

like this. It took me years to work out who I really was and what I wanted to wear. When I was fourteen I looked very conservative and was quite overweight and I didn't fit in. I wish I'd had a friend like you who realised it didn't matter, though. Most of the other kids were pretty mean to me.'

I hesitated. I was about to tell Belinda that I wasn't really friends with Annabel. Three weeks ago I hardly even knew she existed. But the truth was I liked Annabel. I wanted to be friends with her. I just wished she didn't look like such a geek. Argh! I can't believe I just said that. What had I said to Belinda about hating the way people judged you on what you were wearing? I am such a hypocrite.

When we reached Belinda's gate she said I could come in and see if she had any clothes I could borrow. I must have looked confused; she's so much bigger than me.

'It's okay,' she laughed. 'I run an online clothes business. I've got loads of stuff in there. There's bound to be something that will fit you.'

And that's how I ended up in Belinda's flat trying on clothes. It was fun with her. When I go shopping for clothes, I always end up looking at the kids' clothes because I'm so small. I can fit into the eight-to-ten-year-old stuff which is one of the reasons I hate shopping so much.

Their flat was fairly small but really nice. There were interesting things everywhere; sort of like a cross between a museum and a junk shop. I could have spent ages just looking. Even the things that are usually boring, like picture frames, were interesting. Belinda had stuck things onto them. One picture had a feather boa stuck all round the frame and another was made out of cutlery, all sort of melted together into a silver frame, but you could still see that they'd been forks, knives and spoons. There were some big African drums in the corner that they seemed to be using as a table because there was a mug and some leaflets on the top.

Belinda took me into a room at the back that was completely full of clothes except for one corner where there was a desk with a computer on it.

'I've got my own website,' said Belinda, 'but I sell through other websites as well. My website is vintage clothes but really I sell anything. If I see something in a charity shop or at a jumble sale or a boot fair that's cheap and I think I can get more for it, then I buy it.' She smiled and indicated the piles of clothes.

Now I could see that there was some order to the room. On the left was a jumbled pile of clothes and on the right they were neatly folded or hung on rails. There was an ironing board in the middle.

'If I pull something out and you don't like it, just say so,' said Belinda. 'You won't be hurting my feelings or anything. What's important is that you feel good in your clothes.'

By the time Belinda had finished with me I had a brilliant new outfit. We started with the feet and she found a pair of ankle boots in my size, then some leggings and a skirt. I wasn't sure about the skirt at first because I don't usually wear them, but Belinda got me to try it on. It was short, but not too short, and even though it flared out it didn't make me look like a little kid so I kept it on. Then she handed me a top that I thought looked fairly boring until she matched it with a jacket. The jacket was hooded and knitted but it had a strip of fur all round the edges and round the rim of the hood. I fell in love with it at once and decided not to take it off.

I left feeling amazing, and with a huge smile on my face.

When I got home and walked into the kitchen Mum looked impressed.

'Have you been shopping?' she asked.

I told her about my dilemma and how Belinda had helped me.

'Well, I must say, you look nice. If you want I'll buy them for you.'

For the first time ever I was actually looking forward to Wear Your Own Clothes Day.

Saturday 13th November

Mum and Dad went out this morning to get some stuff because Dad's redecorating the spare room.

Chelsea was meant to be looking after us but she disappeared as soon as Mum and Dad had driven away. She knew Spencer and I wouldn't rat on her. I wonder if she knew how relieved we were that she'd gone out.

We were making our lunch, before Annabel was due to arrive, and I was thinking about something that had happened at the end of school on Friday.

I had been getting my things together when I'd heard Stacy say to Lauren in a very loud voice so that I couldn't fail to hear, 'Some people think they're so much better than us. They don't want to associate with us because *we* live on the Ratcliffe estate.'

I was furious. Whose house did she think she was living in?

Who was it that wasn't talking to who?

I was about to say something but they turned their backs on me and Stacy said, 'Come on, Lauren, or we'll be late for choir practice.'

I was still furious about it and I said to Spencer as we ate out toasted sandwiches, 'I'm glad Chelsea dropped that hate campaign against Sophie. I think it's silly that people don't like each other because of where they live or how much money they've got. I thought for a moment that there was going to be an all out battle earlier this term but it seems to have died down now. I haven't heard anything about it for ages.'

Spencer looked at me as if I'd gone mad or sprouted another head or something.

'What?' I said.

'What planet have you been living on?' said Spencer.

'What?' I said again only louder this time. 'What have I missed?'

'I know you're stuck in the servants' quarters but you must have heard the rows that have been going on,' said Spencer.

'No,' I said. I had heard some doors slamming and some raised voices but, once I'm in my room with the door shut and stuck in a good book, the rest of the house might as well not exist. Besides, Chelsea was always slamming doors and shouting.

Spencer was shaking his head and looking at me in disbelief. 'You're seriously telling me you don't know what's going on?'

146

'WHAT?' I shouted. 'Tell me!'

'Okay,' said Spencer. 'Basically, Chelsea has stopped going to school. Mum's doing her nut about it but now Chelsea's sixteen and in the Sixth Form she doesn't have to go.'

'Stopped going to school?' I repeated, moronically.

'Yeah, you know, as in "Not Going".' Spencer said the last two words really slowly like he was explaining to a very dumb person. And I must have looked pretty dumb, sat there with my mouth open.

'Come on,' said Spencer. 'You must have noticed. Or did you think she'd been super-glued to the sofa?'

Now I come to think about it, Chelsea has been either stuck to the sofa or soaking in the new spa bath whenever I'd seen her lately. The trouble is I've been so wrapped up in my own problems I haven't really noticed what anyone else has been doing. That's the problem with living in such a big house. There's no way something so major would have escaped me in the old house.

'Mum's tried everything,' said Spencer. 'She's even cut Chelsea's allowance and threatened to take her phone away and the new laptop she got for her birthday because when she's not watching telly she's on Facebook. I reckon she thinks that because Mum and Dad won the lottery she's not going to need a job, so she doesn't need to go to school. Talk about thick!'

I wanted to agree with him but actually I was quite worried about Chelsea. Was she just going to spend the rest of her life watching television? But what can I do about it? I'm the last person in the world she ever wants to talk to.

Then Annabel arrived and we stopped talking about Chelsea. Annabel and I decided to make some cakes and Spencer thought he'd go and do some homework.

'Your brother's nice,' said Annabel when Spencer had disappeared through the door.

I had to agree with her that, as brothers went, he wasn't bad at all.

When the cakes were cooking in the oven we went outside to explore the garden. It reminded me of the last time Lauren had been here and hadn't wanted to do anything and how I'd worried all the time that she was bored. Annabel was so easy-going I don't think she'd have complained if I'd suggested we cleaned the house.

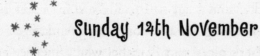

Sunday 14th November

When I woke up I carried on reading one of the books Annabel had lent me and when I finally made it down to the kitchen Mum was looking slightly harassed.

'What's up?' I asked her.

'I know it's only Pam and Gary, and Lauren of course, and they won't mind if everything's not perfect but I would like it to be nice. I never had room at the other house to give dinner parties or anything. I know it's silly to be nervous but I can't help it.'

While I was helping her to peel the vegetables my stomach was churning. Mum wasn't the only one who was nervous. Finally, I was going to get Lauren on her own. I'd get the chance to explain to her about how I came to buy Stacy those clothes. She'd have to listen to me this time – there was no one to butt in.

But I wondered if maybe I should ignore her when she turned up, like she's been ignoring me at school. The trouble is, if Mum noticed she'd be furious and tell me off for being bad-mannered.

I almost told Mum that Lauren and I had fallen out. But then Mum would tell Pam and Pam might tell Lauren off and make her be nice to me and I didn't want someone to be my friend because their mum told them they had to! I let out a huge sigh.

'Goodness,' said Mum, 'whatever's wrong?'

I couldn't tell her about Lauren and Stacy so I ended up telling her about Annabel and her mum and the wheelchair and Annabel doing the shopping and cooking. Mum hadn't met Annabel yesterday when she came round because she'd been out with Dad picking new wallpaper for Morticia's boudoir. I was sort of glad because I didn't want to rub it in that I not only lived in a big, nice house but that I also had a fully functioning mum and a dad and a brother and sister. Which was silly really because there are thousands of people who do, just as there are thousands of people who don't.

Chelsea's not around today, even though Mum made it clear that lunch was a family affair and everyone was expected to be here. No one knows where she's gone but she is going to be in so much trouble when she gets back.

When Lauren was due I went up to Mum and Dad's bedroom to peek out the window at them when they arrived. I'd already told Mum to tell Lauren I was in my bedroom. I thought it would be easier than greeting them at the door because I didn't know how Lauren was going to behave towards me. But when their car drew up in the drive, only Pam and Gary got out. I couldn't believe it. Lauren hadn't even come. All my nervous excitement drained away and left me with a horrible empty feeling.

I went back to my bedroom and curled up on the bean-bag. Ignoring all my new books I picked up the first *Harry Potter*. I'm going to read all of them again. It's nice to lose myself in something familiar that gives me a warm feeling, when nothing else feels right.

Spencer came to get me when it was time for lunch. He saw what I was reading and smiled. Spencer used to love *Harry Potter* as well and a couple of years ago we used to play it all the time. We had an invisibility cloak (an old net curtain) and wands (chopsticks from the takeaway) and a real broomstick Grumps said he'd found in his shed but I think he went out and bought it especially for us. Of course Spencer's too old for those games now, which is a pity because it would be great to play them in this house. I've still got all the things hidden under my bed and sometimes I get out the wand and pretend to cast spells. Though actually I haven't done that since my wishes started to come true. I haven't dared.

When I sat down at the table Pam looked really shocked.

'Charlotte! What are you doing here? I thought you were at that choir thing with Lauren. If I'd known you were going to be here I would have insisted Lauren came, choir or no choir.'

So Lauren hadn't told her mum about us falling out.

'I'm not in the choir, I'm tone deaf – can't sing a note in tune,' I explained, trying to sound cheerful.

'Well, that's very strange,' said Pam. 'I'm certain Lauren said she was going with you. Gary, didn't Lauren say she was going with Charlotte?'

'She certainly said she was meeting her best friend there,' said Gary, helping himself to another roast potato. His hand stopped halfway back to his plate and a sort of stillness descended on everyone round the table as the meaning of that sank in. I was staring at my plateful of food and wishing I wasn't there. And then everyone started talking at the same time. 'This is a lovely meal.' 'Could you pass the carrots, please?' 'Where did you buy the beef?'

Fatally, I looked up and caught Spencer's eye and then we were giggling uncontrollably. Mum didn't tell us off because I think everyone was relieved that the awkward moment had passed. Now I was laughing like a demented person. It was like all the anxiety and embarrassment and uncertainty of the last couple of weeks was bubbling out of me and I couldn't control it. I think Mum was about to say something and even Spencer looked a bit alarmed, but luckily at that moment Chelsea turned up. I knew she'd timed it so she arrived back when Mum's friends were here. That way there was less chance she'd get a rollicking off Mum.

When Spencer and I were clearing the table and taking everything back to the kitchen, I thought how much better I felt now that it was out in the open. It's official: Lauren and I are no longer best friends.

I decided it was time I stopped pretending it wasn't true, and got on with my life. That thought started me giggling again because I sounded like some sort of agony aunt.

'What is wrong with you?' said Spencer.

'Nothing, I'm fine,' I said, and I meant it. I did feel fine. 'By the way,' I continued, '*I've* found a new friend, so how about *you* let up on the studying a bit?'

'Okay,' said Spencer, 'maybe a bit. I might meet Alec down the Games Workshop next Saturday.'

We gave each other a high five, which started me giggling again because it was such a cheesy thing to do but it seemed right somehow.

'The trouble with living in such a big house is that there's about five miles between the dining room and the kitchen,' said Spencer, holding the door open for me. 'In the old house all we had to do was lean over a bit and we could put the dirty plates in the sink without even getting up from the table!'

This was a bit of an exaggeration but I knew what he meant. No wonder people used to have servants. Chelsea was supposed to be helping us but had inevitably disappeared again. Dad and Gary were trying to decide the best place to put the Wi-Fi and Mum and Pam had lit a fire in the sitting room and put their feet up.

I've stayed out of Mum's way this evening because I don't want her questioning me about Lauren. I might be feeling better, but that doesn't mean I want to talk about it.

Wednesday 17th November

I couldn't face the canteen today. I wish I'd thought to take a packed lunch – I figured I'd just go hungry instead.

I've been sitting with a group of girls from my form at lunchtimes. They're friendly and nice, but it's not the same. And, of course, all they want to talk about is the lottery win and what new things have I got and where am I going on holiday.

It made me realise that the only person who's never mentioned money or the lottery to me is Annabel. I never see her in the canteen, though, and I wondered where she went at lunch.

I was planning to go and hide in the loos for the rest of the lunchbreak when I caught sight of a poster advertising a lunch club. *Come and get help with your homework, every day 12.45 – 1.45, Room 122.* Well, it had to be better than the loos and I supposed I could always get help with my maths homework. Especially after the last lesson when Stacy was fooling around and I hardly heard anything the teacher said.

When I opened the door to Room 122 I would have backed out instantly, only someone came up behind me and I was forced to step into the room. I could feel myself going red. I'd only gone and stepped into Geeksville! It was like someone had rounded up every single misfit in the school and herded them into Room 122.

I was about to turn round and escape when one of the bigger, gangly boys approached me. Before he could say anything, a girl shot in front of him. It was Annabel.

'It's okay, Peter,' she said, 'she's with me.'

The boy backed off. 'Make sure she knows the rules, then,' he said, going back to join his friends.

Annabel seemed pleased to see me and found me a chair.

'Couldn't face the canteen, then?' she asked. I wondered if she could read minds.

'What did he mean about rules?' I looked around but there were no teachers in here.

'Oh, don't worry,' said Annabel. 'That's just Peter making sure that the wrong sort don't get in here and start bothering us.'

I looked at her. 'The wrong sort?' I echoed.

'Yeah,' she said matter of factly. 'The rules are that when you're in here you must never say anything horrid about anyone, even the people who have been picking on

156

you. The other rule is that you must not talk about the room to anyone who doesn't use it.'

'But I thought it was here so you could get help with your homework,' I said.

Annabel looked a bit disappointed. 'Did you come in here because you wanted help with homework?'

'Um . . . No, not really,' I admitted.

'Exactly. You came in here because there was someone you wanted to get away from. She Who Shall Not Be Named, or You Know Who.' Annabel smiled at me. 'Sorry,' she said, 'it's just that when I found out about this room last year I felt like Harry Potter must have felt when he discovered the Room of Requirement.'

I had to smile. That was exactly the kind of thought I liked having but would never have dared to say aloud because people would have laughed at me, or looked at me pityingly.

'It was exactly what I needed,' Annabel said, 'a place where I could come and feel safe, where I knew that no one was going to pick on me for one hour in the day.' Annabel didn't sound bitter or cross, just really happy. 'It's okay,' she said, 'you'll be safe in here.'

I felt like I'd entered an alternative universe. One where school wasn't the place you came to meet your friends and have fun despite the lessons, but one where school was an ordeal, where you tried to get through the day without being noticed and picked on.

The truth was, I felt embarrassed being in the room. I

wasn't the victim of bullying. I had to get out of there. I didn't want to be associated with 'the losers'.

Suddenly I felt ashamed of myself. Annabel was really nice, but the truth was I was too embarrassed to be friends with her. I knew that once we left this room the most I would do would be to sit with her in maths and walk up the hill with her. But that was exactly the attitude that had made this room necessary. I also knew that Annabel wouldn't resent me for not associating with her. That made me feel even more ashamed. I wished I was a stronger person and didn't worry so much about what other people thought of me. And in a way, what Stacy and Lauren were doing – being mean and ignoring me – was a form of bullying because it made me feel small. And I had come in here to get away from them. But that didn't make me a loser. I looked around and realised that no one in here was a loser either. It was the people out there who were mean who were the losers.

'Haven't you got any lunch?' said Annabel, looking concerned. 'I've got too much, as usual. Here, have one of my sandwiches.'

I hesitated. I was very hungry. I thought staying for a bit might be okay.

Annabel must have thought I was hesitating out of politeness. 'Go on,' she said, passing me her lunchbox. 'You'll be doing me a favour.'

We spent the next half hour talking about the books I'd borrowed from Annabel.

'You should come to the book club,' she said.
'I think I will,' I told her. And then the bell went.

Thursday 18th November

When I got home today I tried on my new clothes to make sure I had everything right for tomorrow.

Spencer came into my room carrying some bin bags.

'Mum says to put anything you don't want into these and take them down to the hall. She's taking them to the Salvation Army tomorrow.'

I still had a load of stuff I'd brought from my old room which I didn't want any more.

Looking at Spencer standing there in his combat trousers and sweatshirt I thought how much easier it is for boys. No one seems to pay any attention to what they wear. Mostly, *they* don't even pay any attention to what they wear. They are so lucky.

I sorted through all my toys that I'd grown out of. It was hard getting rid of some of the soft toys and I kept some of them. Trevor, my bear, was in my bed as usual. I'd never get rid of him.

The first thing to go into the bin bag was a horrid head thing. I think it was for girls to practise doing hairstyles and make-up on. I couldn't remember ever doing those things with it. I think Spencer and I used to use it for target practice. Next, in went all my old Barbie dolls. Lauren and I had spent hours playing with them. I picked up Barbie Princess and straightened out her skirt. I was pretty sure that this one actually belonged to Lauren. I wondered if she'd want it back. Perhaps I could use it as an excuse to round and see her. I don't want to admit it, but I miss her. I know she's been really horrible to me and I still feel furious at the thought that she wouldn't even listen to my side of the story. I blame Stacy more than Lauren though. It's like Stacy is some evil fairy who's cast a spell of enchantment over Lauren. All I have to do is work out how to break the spell. I pictured myself turning up at Lauren's house with the Barbie doll. She'd think I was mental. Or worse, Stacy would be there and I'd never hear the end of it – about how I still liked to play with Barbie dolls! It would be all over the school in no time. I thrust the Princess Barbie into the bottom of the bag then picked it up and took it downstairs to the hall.

There was already a collection of bags by the front door. From the look of them, Spencer and Chelsea had been doing the same thing. I thought about going through Spencer's bag to see if there were any of his old clothes I could have. But then I decided not to because I have a completely new image now.

And that's when I had a brilliant idea. If I could get Annabel to look a bit more trendy, maybe people wouldn't pick on her so much or write her off as a hopeless geek. Why hadn't I thought of it before? It was so simple. I could hardly take her shopping, though, and buy her a load of new clothes. She'd think I was showing off or trying to buy her friendship or something. Like Lauren thought I'd done with Stacy.

I could see Chelsea's old uniform poking out the top of one of the bin bags. It would be about Annabel's size. School rules say that skirts are meant to be no more than three centimetres above the knee but no one takes any notice and we roll them up at the waistband – in Chelsea's case to about one centimetre below her bum. But even if Annabel doesn't roll it up, Chelsea's old skirt will still be shorter than the one she wears at the moment. I took it out and folded it neatly then put it into a couple of carrier bags. I found Mum in the kitchen.

'I'm just going to see Annabel. I won't be long,' I told her.

I was so excited I practically ran all the way to Annabel's house. Which is why, when I got there and rang the bell, I could hardly speak when Annabel opened the door. I thrust the bags towards her.

'What's this?' she said. She was wearing an apron and was obviously in the middle of cooking tea. I realised that I hadn't really thought about what I was going to say.

162

'Um . . . Chelsea was throwing out her old school uniform and I wondered if you wanted it.'

'I see,' she said. 'Why would I want your sister's old school uniform?'

'Well, I just thought . . .' What could I say? That I could tell her she looked awful in hers? 'I thought . . .'

'You thought that because my mum's in a wheelchair that we're some sort of charity case?' She didn't look at all happy. She was holding a wooden spoon and she started waving it at me. 'Well, we don't want or need your charity. My mum has a very good job as an accountant and we don't need your cast-offs, thanks very much.'

That's right. She thought I was giving her the clothes because I thought she was hard up. I had to explain – I wasn't going to have someone else misunderstanding my motives.

'No, it's not about the money. I didn't think you needed them because of that. It's just that I thought if you looked . . . you know . . . I thought if you looked less . . . well, less like you do, then people might stop picking on you.'

Perhaps I hadn't explained that well enough to not insult her or anything. From the look on her face I didn't think I had. She looked like she was going to hit me with the spoon.

'Who is it, love?' Annabel's mum called from the sitting room.

Annabel glared at me. 'No one,' she called back. 'Absolutely no one,' she said again for my benefit.

I was still holding the bags up. I lowered them slowly.

163

'I thought you were different,' she said to me. 'I thought things like clothes and what people looked like didn't matter to you.' She was looking me up and down and I realised I had my new outfit on. 'Well, I can see that I was wrong. I'm sorry if you're too ashamed of me to be my friend. You don't want me to have these clothes because you think it will stop people laughing at me. You want me to wear them so that you're not too embarrassed to be seen with me! So that people won't laugh at *you* for being my friend.'

'No, that's not it at all . . .' I said desperately.

'If you think I'm going to change just so that you won't be too embarrassed to be seen with me then you're sadly mistaken. I *like* the way I am, okay? Now, if you don't mind, I'm busy.' And she shut the door in my face.

I managed to get home, dump the bags back in the hall and make it up to my room before I started crying.

Friday 19th November

I can't get Annabel's words out of my head. I wondered all night if Annabel was right and I just wanted her to look different for my sake rather than hers. I think it's a bit of both, to be honest. Well, from now on, I was going to be me and I didn't care what I looked like; so this morning I decided I wasn't going to wear the nice new outfit to school today. I'd show Annabel that clothes didn't matter to me.

I looked through my wardrobe and found the clothes I used to wear back in the Ratcliffe estate days. I put on Spencer's old trainers and the turned-up combat trousers and found an old green and brown camouflage top. I felt like a soldier about to go into battle. Which, in a way, I was.

The only thing that clothes had done for me so far was to get me into trouble.

I got Dad to give me a lift to school because I couldn't

face the bus. Or rather, I couldn't face Annabel. I was so embarrassed by what I'd done. I was almost more upset about Annabel not liking me than I was about Lauren not liking me. I thought about pretending I was ill so I didn't have to go into school at all but Mum would see right through that one. She'd know I wasn't really ill and then she'd start questioning me about why I didn't want to go to school and was I being bullied? I decided it would just be simpler to go in and face up to the fact that I didn't have any friends. Who needed friends, anyway? I was fine on my own.

At least that's what I told myself, and I believed it until I walked through the school gates. There was a bit of a buzz in the playground, like there always is on a Wear Your Own Clothes Day. Everyone was talking about what they were wearing and had they seen so-and-so and where did they get that top.

I tried to join in with some of the girls that I'd been having lunch with, but they looked sideways at my outfit and didn't seem too keen to talk to me. I knew it would be different if I'd worn the outfit Belinda had put together for me. God! People were stupid.

And then Lauren and Stacy turned up.

They walked through the gates with their arms linked and they looked practically identical. They were wearing leggings with shorts over the top and boots up to their knees. The boots had quite high heels, I noticed, and couldn't help thinking that they were probably holding onto each other to stop themselves from falling over. They both had white hoodies on and big, gold hoops in their ears. They'd be told to take those off though. They were against school regulations, even on Wear Your Own Clothes Day.

I'd never seen Lauren wearing anything like that before. They must have gone shopping together.

They were walking towards me, both staring at what I was wearing. I held my breath, wondering if they were going to say anything about my outfit. When Stacy saw me she started giggling.

'It's Wear Your *Own* Clothes Day not Wear Some Random *Tramp's* Clothes Day.'

'More like Wear Your Brother's Clothes Day,' laughed Lauren.

I could feel myself going red and willed myself not to cry. I could see Annabel coming. Had she heard? Annabel was wearing her school uniform. Why hadn't I thought of that? She walked past us and said really loudly,

'Yeah, it's definitely *Tramps'* Day,' but she wasn't looking at me, she was looking straight at Stacy and Lauren.

I had to laugh. I couldn't help it. I never thought Annabel had it in her. Stacy opened her mouth to say something, but Lauren grabbed her arm and pulled her through the doors.

I had to sit with them in the form room because we have designated seats, but they didn't talk to me. I might as well not have existed. I kept my head up and tried to look normal, as though I wasn't bothered. Even if it wasn't true.

Annabel is avoiding me. She got on the bus after me but she didn't look my way and, when we got off, she walked straight up the hill and didn't wait for me. I don't think she's ever going to talk to me again.

Dad's putting on a brave face about the fact he hasn't got a job. He says it will give him a chance to do all the jobs around the house but I know it bothers him. I think Mum's having a hard time with Dad and Chelsea home all day. Mum says she tries to get Chelsea to do cleaning jobs around the house, I think in the hope that Chelsea will go back to school just to get out of doing them. But apparently Chelsea just gets abusive and refuses.

I am an outcast. I am such an outcast that even the outcasts have cast me out. In other words, I can't go to Room 122 at lunchtimes because Annabel goes in there and she doesn't want to speak to me.

On Monday, that boy from before told me I couldn't go in, so I took my packed lunch and a book and sat in a toilet cubicle for the whole lunchbreak. It was horrible. I did think about asking Mum if I could go to a different school, but then I thought that might be worse because I'd still have to make new friends and I wouldn't know where anything was and it might not be any better than this one in the end. People would tease me about my height. At least here they're all used to me, whereas at a new school I'd stand out.

I've started going into the library instead of sitting in the loo. Most people avoid the library because the librarian is so scary. I was a bit scared at first, but then I realised she just doesn't like people messing around in there and if, like me, they're interested in the books then she's perfectly nice and helpful. She's pointed out some really good books to me. I can even manage to eat my lunch in there if I'm really careful that she doesn't see me. Sometimes I see Annabel in there doing her homework. I suppose if she gets it done at school she can spend more time with her mum in the evenings.

I've finished all the books she lent me. I ought to take them round to her flat but I haven't dared yet.

Last Saturday I found a really good secondhand bookshop near our house. I wonder if Annabel knows about it. Mum always agrees to buy books online for me, so my bookcases are filling up fast. I love waking up in the morning and seeing all my books on the shelves.

I've spent a lot of time wishing. I've wished that everything will go back to normal. It hasn't. I've wished Stacy would go away. She hasn't. I've wished Annabel would talk to me. So far she hasn't, though I think she smiled at me on the bus the other day. I think Gypsy Ginny's wishes have all run out. The other day I measured myself on the door frame and started screaming because I'd actually grown half an inch! Chelsea came running along the corridor.

'God!' she said when I told her. 'Is that all? I thought you were dying or something.'

I never knew she cared that much. Then she spoilt it by saying, 'Anyhow, you haven't grown, you idiot, it's just because you've got a new carpet with underlay and stuff.'

I'm not going to measure myself again until after Christmas. I've told Mum that if I haven't grown any more by then I want her to take me to the doctor but she thinks I'm being silly. She said that Gran, Grump's wife who died when I was two, was really small and that it's just genetic and there's nothing anyone can do about it.

Thursday 2nd December

When I got home today I dumped my bag in the hall and was about to go to the kitchen to get a drink and a biscuit when the door from the back passage swung open and Chelsea came storming out. 'I hate you!' she shouted over her shoulder and burst into tears.

I flattened myself against the wall to stop her from knocking me down as she stormed past. The door slammed shut as she made her way up the stairs, then it opened again as Dad came hurling past and I had to flatten myself against the wall again.

'And don't think that just because you've walked off that this is the end of it!' he yelled at her. Dad was yelling. My dad. Yelling! Something was badly wrong.

Dad went out the front door, slamming it behind him.

I heard a loud psst above me. I looked up and saw

Spencer peering through the landing rails.

'Up here, quick,' he whispered dramatically.

I glanced longingly towards the kitchen.

'Don't worry,' he called, 'I've got provisions in my room.' He didn't wait but disappeared up the attic stairs and I followed. *He'd better have biscuits*, I thought as I entered his room.

'So what's the problem?' I said, sitting on his swivel chair and spinning myself round. He hates it when I do that because it messes up the height but he didn't say anything about it. He was running his fingers through his fringe which he only does when he's really upset.

'Chelsea.'

'What's she done now?' I said.

Spencer's fringe was sticking up. It was very funny and normally I'd have teased him but I could tell there was something very wrong and I was beginning to get worried.

'There's been the most horrendous row,' Spencer contin-ued quickly.

I shrugged. 'So what's new?'

'No, I mean like World War Three or something. You're lucky you missed it. I think it's been going on all day. Or at least since Mum checked her credit card balance this morning.'

'What are you talking about?' I said, though I could guess what was coming.

'It turns out that Chelsea's been "borrowing" Mum's credit card and spending loads of money at that Health

Spa shop on the high street.'

I knew the one he meant. It was at the top of the hill where I used to part company with Annabel every day, before we fell out. I did think that Chelsea was looking different. I assumed she was going to her friends for hair, nail and make-up sessions. I couldn't help thinking that Chelsea had been behaving really badly ever since Mum won the lottery. Not that she was exactly well behaved before, but she'd never have done anything like this.

'Mum went completely spare,' Spencer said.

'Well, she would, wouldn't she?' I said. 'You know what Mum thinks about stealing. God, why would Chelsea do that? She must have known Mum would find out!'

'I don't know,' said Spencer. 'Maybe she thought Mum's got so much money she wouldn't notice.'

'Then she's more stupid than I suspected,' I told him. 'If anything, Mum's even more careful with money now than she used to be. I think she's worried she's going to spend it all and have to go back to being hard up again. Surely Chelsea must have noticed that? How could she do something like that to Mum?'

'I reckon that somewhere in her little brain she thinks she's entitled to it,' said Spencer.

For a moment we were both silent while we took in the enormity and stupidity of Chelsea's crime.

'Anyway, Dad's grounded her for life and is taking her allowance until she's paid all the money back. When I escaped upstairs he was saying he was seriously thinking about sending her to one of those Brat Camps in America.'

'Why America?' I said. 'Don't they have them here?'

'No, I checked on the internet. You have to live in the desert or the mountains for weeks or months, or at least until you've realised what a complete idiot you're being. The idea is that you can't escape. This country isn't big enough. You'd only have to walk for a few hours before you found a pub, even if they put the camp in the middle of Exmoor or something. Anyhow, Dad was deadly serious. He said her behaviour was impacting on the whole family and that as the eldest she should be setting an example. I think he's worried that you and I are going to start copying her.'

This was a pretty long speech for Spencer. He opened a drawer in his bedside cabinet and handed me a bottle of Coke and a packet of chocolate biscuits. We sat sipping and nibbling and thinking.

After a bit Spencer said, 'Mum's gone to the Health Spa shop to give them a rocket about accepting a credit card off a sixteen-year-old. I think Dad's gone round to see Grumps. Maybe he's hoping for some advice on being a parent.'

I finished the last of my Coke. 'So if everyone's out, why are we hiding away in your room?' I said indignantly.

'Chelsea's still here. I just thought it would be safer up here.'

'Do you think we should go and see if she's all right?' I didn't want to see Chelsea, not after what she'd done, but that didn't stop me worrying about her.

'Are you serious?' said Spencer. 'She'll only shout at us.

175

You can go if you want, but I don't think she wants to see anyone right now. She's probably blubbing and won't let you in anyway.'

I knew he was right so I went to my room to do my homework. I paused on the landing but Chelsea's door was firmly shut and it was ominously quiet. She wasn't playing her music really loud like she usually does when she's upset.

Dinner was tense. Dad was all for hauling Chelsea out of her room and giving her another telling off but Mum said to leave it. She'd come out when she was hungry. I don't know what's going to happen.

Friday 3rd December

It's nearly midnight and the police have just left. Mum's in tears and Dad is pacing. He never used to pace and I don't think it's because there wasn't enough room in the old house. I've never seen Mum cry like this before either and it's really upsetting.

It all started this morning. I was having breakfast when Mum asked me to take some up to Chelsea. I noticed that she waited until Dad had left the room before asking me to do it, because he would have said Chelsea could come down to the kitchen if she was hungry. Mum, on the other hand, is basically too kind-hearted. I could see she was fretting so I took the glass of orange juice and the plate of hot buttered toast without protesting.

When I knocked on Chelsea's door there was no reply, but then it was a bit early for Chelsea. She's always been a late sleeper. I was tempted to just leave the food outside her bedroom door but I was pretty sure Mum hadn't meant for me to do that so, carefully balancing the plate on top of the glass to free up one hand, I opened the door. I hadn't been in Chelsea's room since we looked round the house. The curtains at the big windows were closed so I couldn't see much. I could make out the bed though. 'Chelsea, I've brought you some breakfast,' I said as loudly as I dared. I felt as though I was entering the dragon's lair.

There was no response so I stepped bravely into the room. I was going to leave the food on the bedside table and maybe give her a bit of a shake if I dared. What I hadn't counted on was the piles of clothes and magazines all over the floor. You'd have thought I'd be prepared after sharing a room with her for so long, but my feet got tangled up and I lurched forward. The toast disappeared under the bed and the orange juice plummeted to the floor, falling silently onto a layer of clothes. My first instinct was to put the light on and then I braced myself for the onslaught of bad language I was certain would follow.

Nothing. The bed was empty and the wardrobe door hung open.

I checked the sofa in the sitting room and the new spa bathroom downstairs before I went to Mum. If I thought she'd looked fretful before, that was nothing to how she looked when I told her. She went white and sank into the nearest chair, then jumped straight back out of it and disappeared out the door calling to Dad. A quick search of the house failed to find Chelsea and Mum and Dad ended up in the kitchen trying to think where she would have gone, or when. We tried her mobile but it went straight to voicemail.

Nobody had seen her since the row yesterday. I was kicking myself for not checking on her yesterday afternoon, but I didn't mention how ominously quiet her room had been and how she could have left while Spencer and I were in his room discussing her because Mum looked worried enough as it was.

'She won't have gone far,' said Dad optimistically.

'You'd better get off to school, or you'll be late,' said Mum. 'Perhaps you could ask around and see if anyone's seen her,' she called as I headed out the door.

I had to leg it down the hill so I didn't miss the bus. The last thing I needed was a detention.

Lunchtime was a nightmare. Because of looking for Chelsea this morning and then leaving in a hurry, I'd forgotten my packed lunch. I grabbed a plate of chips in the canteen and looked around for Chelsea's friends. I couldn't see any. *They'll all be in the Sixth Form common room*, I thought dismally. I'd just have to brave it and go in there. The thought was terrifying but I didn't have any choice. I wished I had someone to go with.

Resentment against Lauren built up in my chest. Where was she when I needed her? She wouldn't be terrified of going to the Sixth Form common room. She'd see it as a great excuse for ogling all the Sixth Form boys. I was standing staring madly round, trying to see an empty seat but

179

also trying not to see Lauren and Stacy having their lunch together because I thought that might just tip me over the edge and I'd start crying right in the middle of the canteen.

Then I saw Annabel waving madly. I turned round to see who she was waving at but there was no one behind me. She was definitely waving at me. I went over to her table.

'What's up?' she said.

'I thought you weren't speaking to me.'

'You look really upset. Are you okay?'

I sat down thankfully next to her and started stuffing chips into my mouth.

'I thought you never came in here,' I said to Annabel. Not that I wasn't pleased to see her.

'Sometimes I do, if we've run out of bread at home or I just fancy a change. Where's the fire?' she said, watching my chips disappearing at an alarming rate.

I explained as briefly as possible about Chelsea disappearing. I didn't tell her about Chelsea stealing from my mum because that was too embarrassing, but I explained that I was going to have to go and find her friends to see if anyone had seen her.

'Do you want me to come with you?' asked Annabel. I didn't know what to say. I didn't want to go on my own but what if the Sixth Formers started picking on her? I noticed that her glasses were held together with a bit of sticking plaster – she must have broken them – and her hair was especially greasy today. I could just imagine some of those enormous boys yelling, 'She should have gone to Specsavers' when they saw us coming. I wouldn't know what to do.

I groaned inwardly. No, the Sixth Formers were far more likely to make fun of me because of my size. They'd probably point out it was the Sixth Form block not the Year 6 block or something equally stupid.

I put the last chip in my mouth to give myself time to decide but Annabel had already decided for me.

'Come on,' she said, grabbing her bag, 'let's go and get it over with.'

In the end it wasn't the ordeal I thought it was going to be. Lower School pupils aren't meant to go into the Sixth Form block unless they've got a really good excuse and we had, so I ignored the stares and concentrated on finding Chelsea's friends. Some of the girls from the estate recognised me and said hi, but none of them had seen Chelsea.

'We thought she'd left,' said Cerys. I didn't know how much to let on. I didn't want wild rumours going round the school that Chelsea had run away. Not that they were wild. Still, I didn't want everyone talking about it and asking me questions, so I said lamely, 'I was just wondering if you'd seen her at all, you know, around the estate or anything.' But no one had.

Then I spotted Josh. I knew I had to go and ask him, but he was playing pool with a particularly huge and scary-look-ing boy. It doesn't matter, I thought, I've got this far; I can't give up now. Then Josh looked up and saw me. He appeared puzzled, sort of frowning at me, then he smiled and came sauntering over. He had the most gorgeous smile and I could see what Chelsea saw in him.

'Aren't you Chelsea's little sister?' he said to me. I cringed at the 'little' but let it pass.

'Yes,' I said. I was about to follow up with, 'Have you seen her at all?' when he said,

'Listen, I haven't seen her for ages. Could you do me a favour and give her this?'

He borrowed a pen and some paper off a girl sitting nearby, then scribbled something on it and handed it to me.

'I lost my phone with her number on it. Is she okay? I haven't seen her around.'

'Yeah,' I mumbled noncommittally. 'I'll give her this.'

On the way out I saw Sophie and Amber. Chelsea would hardly have gone running to *them* so I walked straight past.

As Annabel and I made our way across the playing field there was an awkward silence. I was about to apologise to her for the clothes when she got in first.

'Look, I'm really sorry I got so mad when you brought those clothes round.'

'No, it was my fault. I should be saying sorry. It was a stupid thing to do.'

'No, I definitely overreacted. I know you were just trying to be nice. The thing is, I've been thinking about it and you could be right. It might not be the end of the world if I made a bit more of an effort. You know, ditched the long socks or something.'

I couldn't help smiling. 'So what happened to "I like the way I am"?' I asked.

'Well, I do like the way I am, it's just that maybe I don't like the way I look.'

Now I felt guilty. I bet she'd never thought about it until I'd said what I did.

'No one likes the way they look,' I told her, 'and I think you look fine. Very, you know . . . *you*.'

Annabel laughed. 'Okay,' she said, 'point taken. But what about the socks? Do you think I should go for tights?'

Now it was my turn to laugh. 'I am the last person you should be getting fashion tips from, believe me.' Then I had a great idea. 'Oooh, I know. I'll introduce you to my neighbour, Belinda. She'll know exactly what to do!'

'Okay, but don't expect miracles. I don't want a full makeover or anything. But you know . . . it's just there's this boy,' she said, blushing, 'and I think I like him.'

I don't know how I know, but I'm positive she was thinking about Spencer.

'Thanks for helping me,' I said as we entered the main school building.

'That's okay,' she said. 'I'm sorry we didn't find anyone who's seen Chelsea. Your mum must be going spare.'

That reminded me and I sent a quick text to Mum. *No1s seen Chels is she home yet?*

I got a reply straight back, which meant Mum must have been practically sitting on the phone. *Not yet but I'm sure she'll be back soon.* I knew Mum wasn't sure at all but was just trying to put my mind at rest.

Annabel and I went into the form room together for afternoon registration and I had to sit in my usual place at the same table as Lauren and Stacy.

Stacy said, 'I see you've got a new friend, then,' and smirked at Lauren, who giggled. I'd had more than enough for one day so I glared coldly at Lauren and said, 'She's a damn sight better friend than some people.' I noticed that Lauren blushed and looked away and I don't know what Stacy did, because I'd decided that I was never going to look at her again if I could help it and she could go to hell as far as I was concerned.

I hurried home hoping that Chelsea would be there, sitting on the sofa watching telly. But the house was horribly quiet when I got in and I found Mum sitting at the kitchen table with Pam. Pam had obviously come over to give Mum some moral support. I couldn't help thinking that, if things were different, she would have brought Lauren with her and then I'd have had someone to talk to as well.

'Hi, Pam,' I said as cheerily as I could manage. I didn't want to hang around in case they asked me why Lauren and I had fallen out, though I guess they had more important things on their mind.

Dinner was horrid. No one really wanted to eat anything, so Mum did pizza and Spencer and I ate it in front of the telly while Mum and Dad sat in the kitchen with the phone between them on the table. Mum had been ringing

Chelsea's phone all day, but every time it went straight through to voicemail.

By ten o'clock Mum was crying again so Dad decided it was time to involve the police. He rang the station and told them that his daughter was missing, then spent ages giving them details.

A policewoman turned up and took some notes and asked Mum and Dad for a photo.

Spencer and I hung around in the hall, listening in.

I couldn't understand why they weren't being more urgent about getting out there and finding her. Spencer explained that, if it was me that was missing they'd be taking it more seriously, but Chelsea was sixteen and had clearly run away and not been abducted or kidnapped.

'Oh my God,' I said, clutching his arm. He winced. 'What if she has been kidnapped? What if someone kidnapped her because Mum won the lottery?'

Spencer removed my hand. 'She hasn't been kidnapped,' he said firmly. 'Besides, we'd have had a ransom demand by now if she had. She's just gone off in a huff. She'll be back.' He sounded very certain but it didn't help.

'What if she's run off and then someone sees her wandering around and they abduct her?'

'Stop it!' said Spencer. 'She's fine. No one's abducted her.' But I was crying then. I couldn't help it. It was the not knowing that I couldn't stand. Why didn't she just ring up and say she was okay? I'd kill her when she got back for putting us through this.

I could hear the policewoman asking Mum and Dad if Chelsea had ever done anything like this before.

'No,' I heard Mum say. 'Never.'

I thought about the time on holiday when she'd told us she was going bowling then come back to town for the party. Should I tell them about that? But she'd come back that night, hadn't she? It wasn't the same thing at all. I decided not to say anything. I didn't want to get Chelsea into even more trouble.

The policewoman was giving Mum and Dad a load of statistics about how many young people run away every year and how many come home. She said it had only been twenty-four hours and that she'd make sure a description and alert went out to all the divisions in the county. She told them that if we hadn't heard anything by Sunday night it might be worth thinking about telling the media.

I wanted to run in there and shout at her, 'What are you doing? This is my sister you're talking about!' but I didn't and the policewoman left.

Mum told me and Spencer to go to bed.

I couldn't get to sleep. I decided to try reading *The Secret Garden* again. I pulled it out off the bookshelf and leafed through it, trying to find the part where Mary discovers the garden, because that was my favourite bit. Something fell out of it and I picked it up. It was the little piece of card that I'd got out of the fortune machine at Wookey Hole.

'*Your wishes might come true so be careful what you wish for,*' I read out loud.

I stood there staring at it and a dreadful thought began to take shape in my head. What exactly was it that I had wished for?

I grabbed my diary out of the desk drawer and flicked madly through it. I discovered the entry for the day when we'd found out that Mum and Dad had bought this house and Chelsea had spoilt the whole day by being so angry.

I found it there, written in black and white. *I'm fed up with Chelsea and her tantrums. Why does she have to be such a drama queen? She's such a brat. I wish she'd go away. We'd make a much better family without her.*

The truth was staring me in the face but I still didn't want to believe it. I sat down on the edge of the bed. Was it all my fault? If I hadn't made those random wishes would we still be living on the Ratcliffe estate? Would I still be sharing a room with Chelsea? Would Spencer still be at Avon Comp getting beaten up every day?

If that was the case, then Chelsea wouldn't have run away because she'd never have known about the Health Spa shop and she wouldn't have nicked Mum's credit card and got into so much trouble. If we were still living on the estate then Stacy wouldn't have moved into our old house and she might never have come to our school at all.

The diary fell from my hands and landed with a bump on the floor. If only I hadn't made those stupid wishes! Everything is all my fault.

I was going to go and tell Mum and Dad. I was halfway to the door before I stopped myself. What was I going to say? 'Remember when we were on holiday and we went to Wookey Hole? Well, there was this freaky papier mâché gypsy woman and she granted me some wishes, only I've been a bit silly in what I wished for and it's all my fault that Chelsea has gone.'

Yeah, right! As if they weren't worried enough without thinking their youngest daughter had completely lost her mind.

I feel as though my brain is split in two. The front half is telling me that there's no such thing as magic or wishes coming true. I know this for a fact. It's all nonsense. But all the time my front brain is busy denying it, the piece of brain at the back *knows* it's true really – but will pretend it isn't, if it makes the front brain happy.

'I wish Chelsea would come back.' I'm going to repeat this over and over again until I fall asleep.

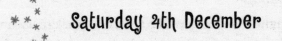

Saturday 4th December

Dad was out again at first light, driving around.

I tried to eat some breakfast. Spencer was in the kitchen; he said he was going to meet Alec. I didn't know what to do. I wished I could be more like Spencer and not worry so much.

When I bit into my toast I suddenly remembered the toast I'd taken up to Chelsea yesterday morning. It was probably still under her bed because I'd forgotten to tell Mum about my accident. Clearing it all up would give me something to do.

Last night the policewoman had asked Mum if Chelsea had taken much with her, in the way of clothes and stuff. Mum had said it was hard to tell because her room was so messy and she'd lost track of what Chelsea had bought since her allowance was raised, though she'd tried to check.

The curtains were open so I didn't trip over again. It must have taken all Mum's self-control not to tidy the room yesterday when she was in here. Chelsea would go mad if she got back and found Mum had gone through her things. No, not *if*, *when*.

I found the toast, butter side down and stuck to a pair of pants. Next I found the glass and felt around the clothes it had fallen on, to see which of them were covered in orange juice. It was when I stood up that I caught sight of the photos. They were pinned onto Chelsea's noticeboard. It was a strip of four from one of those photobooths where you get passport photos. I could see they'd been taken when we were on holiday in Weston-super-Mare because two of them had Zoë in them as well. Chelsea and Zoë were messing around and pulling faces.

And that's when it hit me! The absolute conviction that that's where Chelsea had gone.

I don't know why I was so certain, but all the time Chelsea's been missing I've always thought she must be with someone, because I know she hates being on her own. I was certain she'd gone to Zoë because there was no one else she could have gone to.

I rushed downstairs to tell Mum. Spencer was just leaving. He said Mum had gone to the Health Spa shop to see if Chelsea had been in there. She must have been desperate because that was the last place Chelsea would go after Mum had been in and given them a talking to.

I thought I was going to burst waiting for Mum to get

back. I sat on the stairs and worried. What if Mum thought my idea was mad and refused to check it out? She wouldn't let me go there and see. I knew we could ring the campsite and ask, but Chelsea would have sworn Zoë to secrecy.

I just wanted to go down there and check, to look Zoë in the eye. I'd know if she was lying and had seen Chelsea. Besides, it was all my fault that this had happened so it was up to me to put it right.

I was thinking about getting the train there and not telling Mum until I was sure one way or the other. I didn't want to get her hopes up and then turn out to be wrong. I was about to go upstairs and get my debit card when the doorbell rang. My heart leapt. *It might be Chelsea!* I thought. But when I opened the door it was Belinda standing on the doorstep. She must have seen my expression change from anticipation to disappointment.

'She's not back yet, then?' said Belinda. I shook my head. 'Hey, don't worry, I'm sure she's fine,' Belinda reassured me. Why was everyone so certain? I wanted her to go so that I could get going before Mum got back. I'd leave a note saying I'd gone shopping or something. I didn't want Mum worrying about me as well.

'Is your mum in?' Belinda said. I told her where Mum had gone. 'I'll wait,' said Belinda. She held up a notebook. 'I've got a few ideas for people your mum can contact – charities and organisations who deal with missing persons.'

'She's not missing,' I said, surprising myself at how rude I sounded and then I burst out crying. I was so embarrassed but I couldn't help it. I was desperate to tell her it was all my fault – to come clean – but no one was going to understand.

Belinda was great. She didn't patronise me at all and I ended up telling her about my theory that Chelsea had gone to Weston-super-Mare but how I didn't want to tell Mum in case I'd got it wrong and I thought I'd go and check it out first. She didn't tell me I was mad, or that I couldn't go there on my own, or why didn't I ring them first. She just said, 'Was she very close to this Zoë person?'

'Well, no not really.' I had to admit it, although it didn't do a lot for my argument. 'But then Chelsea isn't really very close to anyone at the moment and I think that's why she might have gone to Zoë – because she won't ask too many questions.'

'You could be right,' said Belinda.

At that moment Mum got back. I could tell she hadn't had any good news the minute she walked in the door. I was praying that Belinda wouldn't say anything about my plans, but she just gave Mum the list she'd made and explained how they might help.

Then Belinda said, 'I have to go out. There's a shop in Weston-super-Mare that's shutting down today and I might get some bargains. I wondered if Charlotte would like to come with me – it might take her mind off things and give you one less thing to worry about.'

I couldn't believe it! I wanted to hug Belinda but I grabbed my coat instead. 'Let's go,' I said, opening the front door.

'Hold on,' said Mum. 'Not so fast.' I thought she was going to say I couldn't go but she only wanted to give me a hug. I was sure she hugged me tighter than usual.

I fell asleep on the way down there because I'd had so little sleep last night. Belinda woke me up when we reached Weston-super-Mare and I directed her to the campsite. We had to drive along the sea-front first because I only knew the way from the pier.

The campsite was still open, despite the fact that it was the middle of winter. But then I remembered that there were a lot of static caravans there. There might even have been people who lived there all the time, for all I knew. Belinda pulled up in front of the reception.

'What's the plan?' she said.

Now we were there, my courage was all gone but I knew I had to do this on my own. It would look odd if a woman was asking for Zoë, whereas I could ask for her without raising any suspicion.

I knocked on the door to the site manager's bungalow. A man opened it. He didn't look very friendly. I swallowed and tried to look and sound as normal as possible, as if I was one of Zoë's school friends calling on her.

'Zoë! Get out here.' The man walked off, back into the bungalow and I waited for Zoë to appear. She came to the door, pulling earphones out of her ears. At first she didn't recognise me, but then I saw it dawn on her and she looked incredibly relieved. She came out, shutting the front door behind her.

'Thank God you're here,' she said, pulling me along the path. Belinda was still sitting in the car and I gave her the thumbs-up as Zoë hurried me past. She nodded and I knew she meant she'd wait for me, wherever it was Zoë was taking me.

'You've got to get her to go home,' Zoë said. 'I've tried but she won't go and I'm going to get into so much trouble if Dad finds out she's here.' I was so relieved I could have sunk down onto the concrete there and then and cried. But Zoë was still dragging me further and further into the caravan park until we reached the very back. There was an old static caravan up against the hedge. Zoë got a key out of her pocket and handed it to me. 'She's in there,' she told me. 'Tell her I can't bring her any more food because my mum's getting suspicious. That should do the trick. And don't be long,' she added, hurrying back towards the bungalow.

I unlocked the door and stepped into the caravan. If anything it was colder in there than it was outside and very gloomy. I guessed Zoë hadn't dared switch the electricity on in case her dad noticed the lights and came to investigate. I saw Chelsea immediately. She was huddled on the sofa, wrapped in a blanket and her nose, which was practically the only bit of her that I could see, was red. Whether it was because she'd been crying or because she was so cold I didn't know.

She didn't move at all but her eyeballs swivelled in my direction.

'Go away,' she said.

I sat down beside her. I didn't know where to start. 'You've got to come home. Mum's worried sick and Dad's driving around trying to find you.'

She didn't say anything but pulled the blanket more tightly around herself.

'Please, Chelsea. You can't stay here. It's freezing. And Zoë says she can't bring you any more food,' I added, remembering Zoë's message. 'Besides, Zoë's terrified her dad's going to find out you're in here and he looks really scary.'

I was certain these weren't the right arguments to get her to come back home but I couldn't think of the right ones. I stuck my hands into my pockets to stop them from getting frostbite.

'Mum and Dad won't be cross any more – they'll just be glad you're back.'

'Dad's going to send me to Brat Camp.' Her voice cracked and she started crying.

'You know Mum would never agree to that,' I said. It was true; I was sure she never would. She believed in sorting out her own problems.

'Is that why you ran away?' I asked. 'Because of Brat Camp?'

'Not only that.' Chelsea sniffed. 'It was everything really.'

'Everything?'

'You know, I was so cross about the house and stuff. I thought when Mum won the lottery everything would change . . . but they're so crap at being millionaires!'

I had to turn away so she didn't see me smile because she was deadly serious.

'And then everything was just the boring old same. We still had to go to school, and Sophie was being horrid about the fact we had loads of money because she couldn't bear the fact I was suddenly richer than her, and then it got difficult with the girls from the estate because I wasn't living there any more and what was the point of school any way? We're millionaires! I just wanted something to happen! That's when I started going to the Health Spa and then I couldn't stop because it made me feel good. You and Spencer were so happy and always giggling and poking fun at me . . . I felt really . . . left out, like nobody liked me. Even the bloody cat doesn't like me! She's always in your room . . .' Chelsea wailed.

'I'm sorry,' I said. 'I didn't realise . . . it's not that Spencer and I don't like you, it's just that . . . well, sometimes you're a bit . . . you know, difficult. We thought *you* didn't like *us*. And you know what Mum's like – she's worried about spending it all and being left with nothing again. She's saving it so that when we leave home she can help us get a flat or house or something and she'll be able to afford for any of us to go to university without a lifetime of debt.'

'I know,' said Chelsea, sounding defeated. 'It's just that I was so disappointed. Sometimes I almost wish Mum hadn't won the lottery.'

'I know what you mean,' I said.

Chelsea looked at me disbelievingly so I tried to explain.

I told her about how Stacy had moved into our old house and taken Lauren away from me and how Spencer had been working too hard because he wasn't as clever as he thought and he hated not being top of the class. I told her how I'd made a really nice new friend and how I'd nearly ruined that because I'd been really rude to her. 'And the worst thing is it's all because Mum won the lottery and it's all my fault!' I said, without thinking. I was crying now.

Chelsea looked alarmed.

'What do you mean, it's your fault?'

So I told her about the trip to Wookey Hole when she'd pretended to be ill and how I'd found the fortune-teller machine and since then loads of my wishes had come true: being able to afford a better holiday next summer, getting to have my own bedroom and Spencer not getting picked on any more. I got so carried away I even told her I'd wished she would go away because she was making everyone's life a misery.

Chelsea made a strangled noise and I thought she was going to shout at me, but when I dared to look at her I saw she was laughing! She was trying to keep it in but it was too much for her and she collapsed sideways onto the sofa, laughing and laughing. At first I was offended and I hit her, but that just made her laugh even more and in the end I was laughing too, because it was so good to see Chelsea laughing again.

I wanted to stop laughing because it was starting to hurt, but every time we tried to stop we'd look at each other and start all over again. I didn't even know why we were laughing.

'What are you laughing at, anyhow?' I said, when we'd finally stopped.

'You!' she said and started laughing again. I hit her again, so she stopped enough to say, 'Sorry, it's just you thinking it's your fault because of the wishes thing. Please tell me you don't still believe in that stuff any more!'

'Of course I don't!' I said as indignantly as possible.

'You do though, don't you? Oh, Charlotte! It hasn't got anything to do with that silly gypsy machine. How could it? Promise me you'll stop blaming yourself.'

'If you promise to come home with me,' I said, 'before Zoë's dad comes and throws us out.'

That brought her back down to earth with a bang. She stood up and peered out the window. 'How did you get here? Are Mum and Dad out there?'

I told her about Belinda giving me a lift. 'You've got to ring Mum and tell her you're okay, though. She's going mad with worry.'

Chelsea pulled her phone out of her pocket. 'Can't,' she said, holding it up. 'The battery died yesterday.'

I wanted to shout at her that she should have rung Mum earlier, and that she hadn't had any sleep last night because of her, and how she'd been crying; but I knew it wasn't the time. I hadn't even got her out of the caravan yet. She could still refuse to come with me.

I got my phone out. 'I'll just let her know you're safe.' I

quickly texted: *Found Chelsea we're on way home*. I hoped it was the truth. I switched the phone off in case Mum rang straight back. I felt bad because I knew Mum would need to talk to Chelsea before her mind was put at rest, but I didn't want her to blow it by mentioning the police or anything that might put Chelsea off going home. I just needed to get Chelsea out to the car. Then I remembered something that might do the trick.

'I saw Josh yesterday. Where's your bag? Did you bring one?'

'You what? Josh? Did he say anything?'

'Yes, he did. Your bag, where is it?'

Chelsea reached down the side of the sofa and pulled out her bag.

'Got everything?' I said.

'Yes,' said Chelsea impatiently. 'What did he say?'

I moved over to the door and opened it. 'He said he'd lost his phone,' I told her, moving outside. She followed desperate to hear more. 'And that he didn't have your number any more,' I said, getting out the key Zoë had given me.

'So that's why he didn't ring,' said Chelsea. 'I knew there had to be a good reason.'

'He wanted me to give you his new number,' I said, locking the caravan door.

'So where is it?' said Chelsea. 'Give it to me. And lend me your phone.'

I bit my tongue. Wasn't it more important that she rang Mum? If I'd been expecting a new, reformed Chelsea I was going to be very disappointed. Some things never change.

'It's at home,' I said, legging it down the path. 'I'll give it you when we get back.'

Chelsea launched herself into the front seat, leaving me to tie up her loose ends. I rang the bell of the bungalow again and breathed a sigh of relief when Zoë opened the door. I wasn't the only one. Zoë sighed with relief when she saw Chelsea in the back of the car. I handed Zoë the key.

'Thanks,' she said and I don't think she was talking about the key, then she shut the door.

I got into the back of the car. I thought the journey home would be one big, awkward silence with Chelsea sulking or being embarrassed in front of Belinda. I couldn't have been more wrong.

'Thanks for bringing Charlotte down here,' Chelsea said to Belinda, all sweetness and light suddenly as if nothing traumatic had ever happened.

'That's okay,' said Belinda. 'I was worried about you.'

Chelsea didn't seem to think there was anything out of the ordinary in that, but I couldn't help wondering why a virtual stranger should worry about Chelsea. It became clear as we were pulling onto the motorway.

'I ran away from home when I was your age,' Belinda said.

Chelsea stopped looking out the window and looked at Belinda. 'Why?' she asked her.

'I was angry,' said Belinda. 'My dad had died and my mum got married again. I didn't like my new step-father.'

'Was he . . . horrid . . . to you?' Chelsea was probably thinking he'd abused her or something.

'No, Colin was a really nice man. If anything, he was nicer than my dad.' She paused, then carried on. 'I think that was one of the reasons I was cross. Also, it seemed so unfair that Mum could just replace her husband so easily whereas I could never replace my dad. If I'd been younger it would have been better because Colin could have been a dad to me, but I was too old for that and I was just cross that mum was so happy. It was completely stupid, but try telling that to a sixteen-year-old,' she said pointedly.

'Where did you go?' asked Chelsea.

'We were living in Coventry and I went to London.'

Oh God, don't give Chelsea ideas, I thought.

'How long did you stick it for?'

'Forever. I never went home.' There was a shocked silence while we took this in. I wanted to tell Belinda to shut up.

'It was the most stupid, most selfish thing I ever did and I truly wish I hadn't done it. I wish I'd been as brave as you and faced the music at home. I'd have saved my mum years of heartbreak and myself from years of misery.'

Chelsea looked uncomfortable at this outburst, but I could also see she was liking the idea that Belinda thought she was being brave.

'I thought about going to London,' said Chelsea, 'but I've heard the stories. I know what it's like.'

'No you don't,' said Belinda. 'You can't know unless

you've lived it. I'm glad you weren't as stupid as me. It took me years to rebuild my relationship with my mother.'

'Did you know Belinda runs a clothes business?' I piped up randomly from the back.

Belinda took the hint and stopped lecturing, which is what Chelsea and I knew she'd been doing even though we didn't doubt it was all true. I knew Chelsea hated being lectured to and might demand to be put down at the nearest bus stop and catch the next bus to London, just to make a point. They spent the rest of the journey talking about Belinda's clothes business.

I think Chelsea must have taken some of it on board though because, when we pulled up in the drive and the front door flew open and Mum came rushing out, Chelsea jumped out the car and let Mum hug all the breath out of her and the first thing she said was, 'I'm really sorry, Mum.'

After school today Annabel came round to my house and I took her next door to meet Belinda. In the end they decided that the best thing would be for Annabel to wear trousers to school. Annabel thought trousers made her bum look big, but Belinda found a pair which really suited her body shape and made her look slimmer. She also said she'd alter Annabel's blazer to look more flattering. That was about it really. If it had been a book or a film or something, Annabel would have come out of Belinda's flat looking amazing and gorgeous and Spencer would have taken one look at her and forgotten all about Emma Lilywhite. Unfortunately it's real life, so Annabel still has her old glasses, though they've been mended now, and ginger hair which Belinda said wasn't ginger at all but copper and totally stunning. Belinda also suggested, really subtly, that Annabel should wash it more often.

I walked Annabel back to her flat and we had a good laugh at ourselves on the way.

'And there was me thinking we weren't interested in clothes,' said Annabel, swinging the bag Belinda had given her to put her new trousers in.

'From this moment on we will never mention clothes again,' I told her firmly.

Everything had just settled down when Mum decided to go overboard on Christmas.

When I got home from school yesterday there was the most enormous tree in the hall. It reached right up to the landing and smelt lovely. Mum decided we needed completely new decorations so I went shopping with her today.

She's organising a big party for Christmas Eve. She's invited all our old friends from the estate and the new ones we've made here, like Belinda and Chris next door and the woman who runs the Health Spa shop. I know! I couldn't believe it either.

After I got Chelsea home, Mum, Dad and Chelsea sat down and had a big talk.

Mum made it clear that Chelsea still had to pay the money back and she had to go back to school. I thought there was going to be a huge argument again and that Chelsea would run away again, but they worked it out. Mum said Chelsea didn't have to go back to Avon Comp, she could go to the Sixth Form college instead. There was a course on beauty therapy that Mum thought would suit Chelsea down to the ground. If it didn't she could pick another course, but she wasn't leaving school at sixteen and ruining her chances of a good job.

Chelsea's now got a part-time job at the Health Spa shop to help pay Mum back.

'It's not the money,' said Mum, 'it's the principle' – whatever that means – 'and it won't do Chelsea any harm to learn the meaning of money.' I know that as far as Chelsea's concerned the only meaning money has is in the spending, but I didn't point that out to Mum. Anyhow, that's how Mum got friendly with Bev from the Health Spa.

I've invited Annabel and her mum to the party. When we were out shopping today, I saw a gorgeous charm bracelet and persuaded Mum to lend me the money so I could buy it for Annabel. I know she'll love it. I bought some charms to go on it. There's a little book, a heart with *friends* written on it, a penguin – because Annabel loves them – and a tiny bell that actually rings. She can buy more if she wants; they're not too expensive.

Grumps is coming, of course, and Uncle Ron and even Auntie Sheila, if she doesn't get one of her headaches again.

Spencer's invited Alec and a couple of boys from his new school. I envy the way Spencer doesn't seem to have a problem mixing his old life with his new one. I couldn't imagine what would happen if I invited Lauren and Annabel.

Josh is coming because he and Chelsea are going out together. I nearly pointed out to her that he might have a smile to die for, but she *did* find him snogging Sophie at the hot-tub party last summer, so perhaps he isn't to be totally trusted. But Chelsea is so happy about it I decided to keep my mouth shut.

Naturally, Pam and Gary are coming, but I'm pretty sure Lauren will find she's absolutely just got to be somewhere else, so I'm not worried about that.

Chelsea's helping Mum with the party and is still trying to persuade her to get outside caterers in, but Mum says it would look like we were showing off if there were waiters wandering around. She has promised to buy all the food in from Marks and Spencer though.

Chelsea's been a lot easier to live with since she came back. I'd like to think she realises she was behaving like a spoilt brat but I know it's really because she's finally got her hands on Josh.

Friday 24th December

The most amazing thing happened tonight, although it wasn't so much 'the thing' that was amazing as my reaction to it.

The party was in full swing and Annabel and I decided to grab some food and take it up to my room. There was a new book I wanted to show her and I had to give her the present as well.

Spencer was in charge of the music and he'd just put some really corny Christmas songs on. 'Do they know it's Christmas?' was playing as we went up the stairs.

'More to the point, do they care?' said Annabel. I had to laugh. She was right; it might be a charity song to help the victims of famine in Africa, but why would they care about Christmas when they were starving? That was the thing I liked best about Annabel. She didn't take anything for granted and always made me see things in a different way.

We found Missy sitting on my bed, keeping out of the way of all the noise and feet downstairs. Annabel made a fuss of her while I found the book I wanted to show her.

We'd just finished eating all the food when there was a knock on my bedroom door.

The door opened and Lauren walked in. 'Your mum said you were up here.'

I just stared at her. She began to look a bit uncomfortable. Annabel got up and muttered something about going to check on her mum. Missy followed her out the door and I noticed her tail was twitching. She doesn't like strangers.

Lauren plonked herself down on the beanbag that Annabel had just left. I don't think she'd even registered that Annabel was there and it made me angry. I realised I still hadn't said anything but I didn't know what to say. I hadn't spoken to Lauren for weeks.

Lauren was shifting about in the beanbag trying to get comfortable. They're meant for relaxing in and she was looking far from relaxed.

'Look,' said Lauren, 'I want to apologise. I've been really mean. I don't know why.'

I still couldn't think what to say. Apart from, 'Yes, you have, now go away.' But I didn't, so Lauren carried on.

'The thing is . . . I don't know . . . I think I was cross with you for moving away. And then Stacy came.' She paused, trying to find the right words. 'It was all her fault really.'

I wasn't sure those were the right words. How could it be

all Stacy's fault? Lauren had been there too. She'd chosen to be mean as well.

Lauren seemed to realise what she'd said.

'No, I mean . . . of course it was my fault, but Stacy told me you were slagging me off when you were in maths together and that you weren't sure you wanted to associate with people from the estate, now you were rich and everything, and then you went and bought her all those new clothes and I thought you were trying to buy her friendship and wanted to be friends with her instead of me.' Lauren stopped to draw breath.

I shut my mouth because it was hanging open.

'And you believed her?' I asked, with as much outrage as I could.

'She's very persuasive,' said Lauren. 'Then I went shopping with her and she nicked some stuff. I thought we were going to get caught.'

'So you believe me now? About me buying those things for her so she didn't steal them?'

'I *knew* it was true,' shrieked Lauren. 'She swore you insisted on getting them for her. She said you wanted to show off about how much money you had.'

I wanted to shout at her. Why hadn't she listened to me, not Stacy? Then none of this would have happened.

Lauren carried on, 'I've really missed being friends with you. Stacy isn't the same. She's only interested in boys and make-up and stuff, and what people are wearing. When she came over for the night, all she wanted to do was go on

Facebook all the time. And when I suggested a film she only wanted to watch horror movies which I hate. Please, Charlotte, can we be friends again? Best friends, best friends whatever, best friends forever.'

A vision of Spencer pretending to stick his fingers down his throat and throw up popped into my head. It was only a few months ago that we'd made that pact, but it felt like a lifetime away and now it sounded really silly.

'Okay,' I said.

Lauren shrieked and threw her arms round me. 'Really? Do you mean it?'

A part of me wanted to tell Lauren that I didn't want to be her friend any more because she'd hurt me too much. I wanted to hurt her back. But another part of me wanted nothing more than to be friends like we used to be. Lauren was so familiar she was almost like a sister. And I knew, from having Chelsea as a sister, that even though you don't nec- essarily like them all the time, you can't help loving them.

There was just one thing I needed to know.

'What about Stacy?' I said. 'I don't want her hanging around. I can't stand her.'

Lauren was fiddling with the ornaments on my mantel- piece.

'Oh, don't worry about that,' she said. 'Stacy won't even be at school next term. She's moving back to London. Her mum doesn't like it here.'

I wanted to shout and scream. Lauren didn't want to be friends with me again because she'd missed me! She just didn't want to be alone when her precious Stacy went back to London. I was about to tell her I'd changed my mind and she could go to hell, but she'd picked up the present I'd bought for Annabel which I'd left on the mantelpiece and had been about to give to Annabel when Lauren had come in. She was reading the label tied to it. I'd written: *To the best friend a girl could have.*

'Is this for me?' said Lauren.

She had to be joking! I grabbed the present out of her hand. Lauren looked startled. I guess I had what Spencer calls 'the rabid tiger' look on my face. She took a step backwards.

'Can't you read?' I said. 'It says – *To the best friend a girl could have* – and the last time I looked that wasn't you.'

'So who is it for then?' said Lauren.

'I bought this for Annabel,' I told her.

She looked confused for a moment. 'What, Annabel as in the fat geeky girl? Why?'

'In case you haven't noticed,' I said through gritted teeth, 'things haven't been too easy for me just lately and Annabel, who isn't fat by the way or in any way geeky, has been there for me when I needed her.' I finished pointedly.

Lauren looked guilty, but only for a nanosecond. 'Things can't have been that bad,' she said. 'I mean your mum won the lottery for God's sake! How hard can that be?'

The compulsion to scream finally got the better of me. When I'd finished I carefully put the present back on the mantelpiece and turned to Lauren.

'Well,' I said, a lot more calmly than I was feeling, 'Dad lost his job which he loved, Spencer had trouble getting used to his new school, Chelsea ... well, let's just say Chelsea ran away and I had to chase halfway across the country looking for her,' this was an exaggeration, obviously, but I was getting into my stride now, 'and I had to move away from my best friend!' I hoped I didn't sound too much like a 'poor little rich girl' so I carried on quickly.

'The worst thing is – I could have coped with all that – if my so-called best friend hadn't deserted me and started being horrible for no better reason than my mum just happened to win the lottery.'

'That wasn't the reason!' said Lauren.

'Well, what was the reason then? I'm dying to know. And don't tell me it was because I changed because I didn't.'

Lauren didn't say anything for a full minute.

'Okay,' she said finally, 'I admit I was jealous of you, moving here to this big house – and I know it was silly of me – but I was cross with you for moving, even though it wasn't your fault, and then Stacy came along ...'

'And you decided you didn't need me any more?'

'It was all those things she said about you. I thought they were true.'

'A true friend would have asked me. A true friend wouldn't have believed them in the first place ...' I didn't want to go on, I was tired of all this. I wanted to go and find Annabel and give her the present.

'Look,' I said. 'It doesn't matter. I know what Stacy's like but I can't believe you were taken in by her. I'm glad she's going back to London. Good riddance to her. If you want to hang out with me and Annabel when we go back to school then that's fine, but if you can't accept her then you'll have to do without me.'

Lauren opened her mouth to say something but I didn't want to hear any more.

'I'm going downstairs now, there's a party on,' I said, then I walked out and left her standing there.

I know our friendship will never be the same again but I don't want us to be enemies. All the same, there is a tiny part of me that's hoping that she won't want to hang out with me and Annabel.

Sunday 26th December

Christmas Day was totally mental. I think Mum and Dad were trying to make up for all the years they hadn't been able to afford to give us much.

I got a computer, all to myself, and a huge heap of other stuff, including a new MP3 player and a smartphone.

Spencer got a new bike and a heap of War Hammer stuff and Chelsea got money so she could get the things she wanted for herself.

Mum told Chelsea she couldn't use any of it to pay her back. She had to earn the money she owed. Chelsea didn't mind. She loves her new job at the Health Spa.

They also bought us all a Nintendo Wii and a load of games we could play on it together.

Missy got a new collar with diamonds on it. Not real ones, obviously. Mum hasn't lost her mind.

Grumps got a new pair of slippers, because that's what he always gets and Dad said he'd be unhappy with anything else.

Just when we thought it couldn't get any better Mum handed us all an envelope. Chelsea ripped hers open and started screaming. I tore mine open to see what all the fuss was about and inside was a piece of paper with *One Holiday to Florida* written on it. Mum brought out a load of brochures about all the things we could do when we got there. Chelsea made a grab for them then chucked one to me. It was for *The Wizarding World of Harry Potter*.

All the stuff – the computer and the holiday and the phone and the MP3 player – is great but, if anyone asks me, the best thing about winning the lottery is that you really know who your friends are. And to think that if it wasn't for the lottery I would never even have spoken to Annabel.

Chelsea just came into my bedroom. She's never been in here before.

She's been teasing me mercilessly about the wishes thing ever since our chat in the caravan. I think it's pretty mean of her, considering it was me who went and rescued her.

She looked around at my new bed and the huge bookcase with all the books and the beanbags and the fireplace and blue flowery wallpaper.

'Hmm,' she said eventually, 'it's very . . . you.' She paused. 'It's nice, I like it.' Which is as much of a compliment as I'm ever going to get off her.

'I've been thinking,' she said, 'in case you're still worried about the wishes and everything being your fault . . .'

I wondered how she knew that I still worried about how I had to be careful about what I thought in case I accidentally made a wish I didn't mean.

'. . . Well, if you think about it, everything happened because Mum won the lottery; us moving – which meant you got your own room and Spencer went to a new school and all that stuff with me – and don't start thinking that Mum won the lottery just so all those wishes could come true, because technically Mum won the lottery before we went on holiday and before you went anywhere near that gypsy machine. I just thought you should know because I bet you're still worrying, so stop it.' And then she left.

So I've decided to put all that magic nonsense behind me from now on. At least that's what the front part of my brain is thinking. I'm trying to ignore the bit at the back.

Spencer bought me a new diary for Christmas. I didn't have the heart to tell him that I'm not going to write one any more. I don't really need to. One of the reasons I kept this one was because I needed to put down all my crazy thoughts, the sort that Lauren said were my imagination getting carried away. Well, now I can share them with Annabel because she has them too and she doesn't think I'm deranged.

I gave Annabel the bracelet and she loves it. I'm going to get one for myself and every time the little bell charm rings it will remind me how important it is to be loyal to your friends.

217

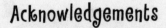

Acknowledgements

I would like to thank Phil for doing all the boring things so I don't have to, and George, who keeps me sane by making me laugh insanely.

Thanks to my editor Anne for all her hard work and to my friend Dawn for her continuing support. Also, thanks go to my three sisters who encourage me when it's most needed.

Alice in time

PENELOPE BUSH

If you could revisit your past, what would you see?

Things are at crisis point for fourteen-year-old Alice. Her mum is ruining her life, her dad's getting remarried, and Sasha, the most popular girl in school, hates her guts . . .

Then a bizarre accident happens, and Alice finds herself re-living her life as a seven-year-old through teenage eyes – and discovering some awkward truths. But can she use her new knowledge to change her own future?

'An amazing book.
Cleverly written, exciting and fast-paced.'
Chicklish

'An ambitious and successful novel.'
Books for Keeps